JESSICA WATKINS PRESENTS

LONG AS
YOU
KNOW WHO YOU
Belong To

BRI NOREEN

Prologue

I watched as the glass vase I had been holding in my hand soared through the air, crashed landed against the white croc skin wallpaper, and burst into a million pieces. Tears rained down my disfigured face, burning my open wounds as I tried to come to grips with what had just happened.

"Ma'am …you're not in any condition to be moving around," the nurse timidly stated. I whipped around so forcefully that my neck made a popping noise.

"Bitch, if you don't get the fuck out my business, you're going to be the next thing that goes flying across this fucking room. Now piss off!" I roared. Without another word, she ran her ass up out the room, heeding my warning.

"How could this have happened? Why would he do this?" I dropped to my knees and landed right on a pile of broken glass. The glass cut into my flesh, immediately causing blood to leak all over the mahogany wood floors. The pain of the open wounds felt like the cusp of an orgasm in comparison to the unbearable pain I felt in my heart.

Rage wasn't a strong enough word to describe the feeling coursing through my body. It was something worse than that. Deadlier than that. The feeling was consuming me, eating me alive from the inside out. It was awakening a dark side of me that no one, including me, had ever borne witness to.

Stumbling, I rose from the broken glass and limped to my room. During the short trip from the mirror to my bed, I thought about the possible ways I could make him suffer twelve times over. Letting gunshots ring off and hit his body like Fourth of July fireworks wouldn't be satisfying enough. Drawing blood by stabbing him directly in the heart as he had stabbed me—metaphorically speaking, of course—would be too swift. No, he needed to be dealt with in a specific manner. He needed to have everything in his life stripped from him and be forced to live with the daily reminder that he was the one that brought this on himself. The gauntlet had been thrown, and I wasn't going to stop until the nigga that I'd given my heart to had his ripped out and hung on a wall like a trophy of vengeance won.

Nakami

May 2014

"You're a fucking idiot!" I screamed so loud that my own eardrums popped. Tristan stood in front of me frozen with fear, and she had every right to piss her pants right now. If I had been armed, her family would have needed a closed casket goodbye.

"I told you what to order. I wrote it down. I spelled it out. I practically wrote the order myself, and you still managed to fuck this up!" I could feel my face turning a vivid shade of red; a sure sign that rage had taken over my body. I couldn't tell if Tristan was shaking, or if I was and that was why it seemed as if she was moving. But I didn't care which was happening.

"I...I didn't touch the order. I sent it in as you gave it to me," she stuttered.

My leopard print Charlotte Olympia pumps made sweet music against the hardwood floors as I strutted over to where Tristan stood. I got so close to her that I could probably write the menu of what she had for lunch by the smell of her breath.

"Are you trying to tell me that *I* made the mistake?"

"That's not what I said!" she screeched.

"Get out my face. Now!" I yelled.

Tristan scurried away like a terrified rat. I closed the door angrily, causing the expensive pictures on the wall to rattle. I wanted to fire her. I needed to fire her. But I couldn't. She would be the sixth assistant that I had gotten rid of in three weeks, and my schedule was too tight. I just couldn't go through the hassle of putting up an ad and sifting through resumes, only to hire someone as incompetent as the ones that had come before her. I just didn't understand why no one could get this right!

I pulled out my phone to call my father, but I changed my mind before I could get it all the way out of my purse. One thing I didn't want to hear was him calling me Kamikaze because of my reckless attitude. It was his little pet name for me that had developed because of my outrageous temper tantrums. On top of it describing me well, it also was a blend of my name and my mother's.

My birth name was Nakami Yukimura. I was born to my Japanese father, Hironori Yukimura, better known in the streets as Hero, and my African-American mother, Kazira Prince. My dad told me that I was the spitting image of her. The only features I'd stolen from him were my chinky light brown eyes. My honey brown skin complexion, my wavy brown tresses, my stacked body, and my long lashes were definitely gifts from my mother. I hadn't been fortunate enough to know her because she'd died while giving birth to me, but my father had enough pictures and stories for me to build a concrete image of her in my head.

The love I had for my father ran deep. He'd had it rough trying to raise a daughter and run a drug empire, but he'd been successful in both arenas. I idolized him, and whatever he said was law. I'd never put anyone or anything before him, and I never planned to do so. I'd followed his orders when he told me to put school above boys and parties, and I'd graduated from UCLA with a degree in Business Management on his orders. This was why I moved into the city and out of the hills to run my event planning business. Well, although it *was* my business, it was just a way to legally clean my father's drug money. My heart was telling me that he was trying to get out of the drug business and clean as much money as possible. But whatever he wanted, I was down for it. A ride or die bitch didn't have to be a girl riding for her man. I was definitely a ride or die bitch for my father.

"Your new client, Mr. Summers, is here," Tristan poked her head into my office and said. Her voice was barely above a whisper.

"Ugh," I groaned.

I just needed a moment to myself. I had forgotten all about the new client I was supposed to be planning for. He was referred to me by another wealthy client of mine, so I knew that I needed to man up, put my game face on, and handle my business. I waved Tristan off and stood from my desk. I walked over to my mirror to take a good look at myself and make sure that I was at my best.

Standing 5'7" without heels, my super thick frame looked even more svelte and balanced with my favorite pair of designer pumps that gave me an extra 6 inches of height. My long, thick mane was wand curled to perfection and cascaded down my back, and my little baby hairs were extra popping. I was dressed in a cobalt blue Alice + Olivia bodycon dress with a deep-v in the front, as well as a modest split. The dress hugged my wide, child bearing hips, 36D breasts, and round ass like it was made with only my body in mind.

My face was flawless; my chinky bedroom eyes were framed by long, dark lashes, my caramel skin sparkled with 24k gold bronzer, and my full lips were coated with Lime Crime's Velvetine Salem lip color. People often told me that my face reminded them of the actress and model Tae Heckard, but my body was more Serena Williams. Whatever. I looked better than any bitch on TV.

Satisfied with how I looked, the only decision left was whether I should throw on my blazer or no. Since I was meeting with a man, I figured the more skin, the better. So I left the blazer on the back of my office chair.

Taking a deep breath, I walked out of my office to greet my new client.

Got. Damn.

Standing at least 6'3", with skin the color of vanilla bean ice cream, sandy brown neatly twisted dreads, a full beard and mustache of the same color, and cool grey eyes, Mr. Summers took my breath and my heart in two seconds flat. I blushed hard when he casually threw a smile my way, revealing his deep-set dimples. My GAWD this man was gorgeous! Dressed in Balmain Moto Jeans, a white v-neck t-shirt, black and grey Giuseppe Zanotti high-top sneakers, and a grey color block Lanvin button down cardigan, this man had my heart palpitating before he could even speak a word.

"I take it that you're Nakami. Not to be unprofessional, but damn you're gorgeous," his deep voice boomed, instantly making my body quiver and my juice box leak. He extended his hand for me to shake. I obliged.

"I am. Nice to meet you, Mr. Summers. And thank you for the compliment."

"It's Kendrick. Mr. Summers is a greeting for somebody much older than I am," he laughed. "Or my friends call me Grey. That is, if you plan on becoming my friend," he teased.

"The way you're staring at me, it's hard not to imagine we'll eventually become more than that," I replied. He raised his eyebrow and smirked in amusement. "But let's stick to business for now, Kendrick."

He was planning a grand opening party for his new club, South Beach. The club sounded amazing and completely different than anything I'd ever seen or heard of. For the grand opening, he wanted to stick to the Miami theme, and I had less than two weeks to pull it together. Talk about pressure. And although Grey...my bad, Kendrick...was easy on the eyes, I could tell that his demanding ass was not going to be easy to please. I had my work cut out for me. But for a man that damn fine, I was willing to lose some sleep and slay some dragons to satisfy him. All I knew was that after this party, not only was I going to end up with a $200K check in my account, I was going to end up with a new man in my life.

GREY

May 2014

This legit shit was starting to wear thin on my nerves. I was ready to get back to the fucking hustle. Uprooting my life and hopping my ass all the way across the country, from Detroit to LA, had never even crossed my mind. But I don't back down from a challenge. So when my connect, Jorge Nueva, was busted by the DEA and the Feds, I got ghost before they locked my ass down too. I dropped everything but the cash in my safe, which amounted to a little over $3 million. I knew that the shit wouldn't last long. But I was born on a dollar and a dream, so I knew I could make it do what it do.

The first thing I did when I touched down in Los Angeles four months ago was find out what the hot shit was here. My nigga, Tyler, had made the move with me, and it only took him two weeks to get back to the money. But I wasn't a corporate nigga. Tyler was an engineer with mad skills. Even though I had earned my Bachelor's as well, I could never see myself working some weak ass 9 to 5. So because I needed time to figure out how to get into the drug game out west, I had to find some kind of business that was going to keep my money flowing in the meantime.

Being the home to the stars, it was really a no-brainer to open a club. But the list of clubs in Hollywood and Beverly Hills was long, and the clubs were definitely official; none of that bullshit that you get when you come to the D. These clubs in LA brought out the music business' most elite players, Hollywood's A-list actors, and the world's most famous athletes. So I knew I had to come with it in order to make shit pop. But that ain't a thing. A nigga is real creative, so I knew South Beach would be on the top of every website's top ten list in a matter of months. But all the bullshit that came with opening a club was for the birds. Permits, licenses, ordering the liquor, hiring the staff, meeting with the interior designer, strategizing with a marketing team, sending out invites to PR people...Like, damn! Can't I just buy the space and open that bitch already?

I sighed out loud just thinking about it. The only good thing that came out of it was Nakami's fine ass. Baby girl was fire, and she knew it. I'd heard about ol' girl though; heard that attitude was something fierce and that she was as lethal as snake venom. But it was all good. I had nine inches of get right that I knew would put that ass in place. I walked out of her office trying to talk my dick out of walking back in there and bending her ass over that desk.

Thankfully, my phone rung and averted my attention. "Little bro. What did I do to deserve this phone call?"

"Man, please tell me that it ain't true. Please tell me you ain't out here in LA?"

"So much for the welcome wagon, huh my nigga?" I half joked.

"C'mon, Grey! Why you couldn't stay your ass in Detroit?" He sounded pissed, and that made me irritated.

"Nigga, are you serious? You should be popping a bottle, putting me up on one of them model bitches you roll with, and showing me around town…not whining into my damn phone! Fuck wrong with you?"

"You know what the fuck is wrong with me. I'm out here trying to leave that ghetto shit in the past, and you come out here to my city dragging it with you!"

Let me explain something about my brother. This ain't how it always was between us. Me and Kimani used to be so tight that people thought we were fraternal twins. We ran the halls of school as well as the streets together, and you rarely saw one without the other. But after Kimani's girlfriend, Ginae, got killed during a shootout with a rival drug family, Kimani turned bitch and dipped from the city. He moved to California a day after her funeral without saying two fucking words to me, and he never looked back. Now his modeling ass thought he was the shit because his dick print was posted on billboards and in magazines. Fuck outta here. He was still "Mani from Highland Park" to me.

"Aye, you the one calling me. Not the other way around," I told him. "I left you out of it."

"I don't need this right now. I got my agent trying to line up acting gigs and…"

"Oh, so you an old Christian Keyes, Morris Chestnut, and Michael Ealy looking ass nigga now?" I burst out laughing just imagining his ass trying to act.

"Laugh if you want to, but at least I'm legit."

"So am I, fool," I boasted.

"What? Fuck you talm'bout?"

"I'm opening a club. In Hollywood. Next week actually. And I got a bad bitch throwing the grand opening party. I got celebrities coming out, and Big Sean's DJ, Mo Beatz, is djing that shit, bro."

Silence was all I heard on the phone. My brother wasn't stupid. He knew that being legit was a necessity but that hustling was where my heart was and that, even though I might not be doing it at the moment, it wouldn't be much longer before I found a way to get my hands into something illegal.

"Is that right?" he finally replied.

"Yeah, man. So if your ol' Hollywood ass ain't got nothing to do next week, come through the spot."

"Look, man. I got an image now. I can't be caught up in no bullshit."

"Ok, so when some bullshit comes up, I'll keep you out of it. Just come parlay with your big brother, man. Shit."

I heard Kimani sigh loudly through the phone before he spoke again. "Aight, man. I'll be through there."

"Bet."

I ended the call and hopped into my pearl white 2014 Tesla Model S and tossed my phone into the passenger seat. Today hadn't been all that bad. The straight and narrow shit was cool for the time being, but my hands were itching to get into some trouble. To hell with that shit my brother was talking.

NAKAMI

May 2014

"Where are the rest of the bird of paradise flowers we ordered?" I surprised myself with the moderate volume yell that came out of my mouth. I guess the Xanax was really working.

"They're in the back. I'm going to grab them right now." Tristan scurried past me before I could get another word out.

It was the grand opening night of South Beach, and all hands were on deck. I was dressed in a comfy Helmut Lang jumpsuit, and I was wearing gold and snakeskin Isabel Marant sneaker wedges. My wet, curly hair had been haphazardly thrown into a top knot. I was not above jumping in and dripping a little sweat in order for my reputation as the ultimate event planner to remain intact. And in this case, everything needed to be exceptional because I was hell bent on impressing Grey. I went to make sure that the alcohol had been situated at the bar the way that I specified and was stopped by a mail courier.

"Ms. Yukimura?"

"Yes, what is it?" I asked curtly.

"I have a package for you. Please sign here."

The courier extended his clipboard and handed me a pen. Draped over his shoulder was a large garment bag from Nordstrom. I signed quickly, and the courier handed me the garment bag as well as a shopping bag. He smiled and went on his merry way, leaving me super confused. Attached to the garment bag was a card. Curious, I snatched it off and laid the other items on top of the bar.

Work ends now. I know that this place is going to look just how I envisioned it. So take your pretty ass to 9641 Sunset Boulevard and unwind. You're my date tonight.

-Grey

I couldn't contain my smile. I really thought I was going to have to put in work to get his ass, but clearly I'd done something right in the two weeks I'd known Grey. We'd worked closely on getting everything ready for the grand opening, but he had made sure that we remained professional. But now, not only was he staking his claim, but he was also showering me with gifts, and I hadn't even given him a taste of the good stuff yet. I looked around at the club and decided that I couldn't leave right away. Even though I'd managed to snag Grey for the night, I knew he wasn't the type whose attention and interest was easy to maintain. This party still needed to go off without a hitch.

An hour later, I walked out of the club and drove my custom painted, plum colored Porsche Boxster GTS to the Beverly Hills Hotel as the card instructed. When I arrived, the desk clerk let me know that I was booked in the Presidential Bungalow Suite. This nigga had really gone out his way! As soon as I approached the door to my suite, I remembered I was at this hotel without my essentials: my wand curler, my Carol's Daughter hair products, my extensive make-up collection, and my Jo Malone Red Roses Body Wash. I used my key and entered the room anyway, figuring I would set my things down and run back to my loft. Two seconds after I closed the door, there was a knock.

I opened it and in barged a heavy set woman with a large silver case and a rolling suit case, a tall slender model-like man with a super beat face, and a fumbling mess of a young girl looking as though she was going to fall over from the weight of the things she was carrying in her hands.

"Excuse the fuck outta me? Who the hell are ya'll, and why are you in my suite?" I stopped them in the hallway before they could get any further.

"Uh-uh, boo. TyTy don't do attitudes. I came up in here to beat a face, not beat some ass, but I will not hesitate to throw dem hands, honey," the man said.

"Do what you gotta do, but first you gon' tell me what you doing up in my suite!" I wasn't going to let up.

"I'm Princess." Princess extended her hand to me and I looked at that shit like it was drenched in Ebola. She continued. "That's Tyrell, or TyTy as he likes to be called. And that's Lola, our assistant."

"Again, the fuck are ya'll doing in my suite?" I didn't know if these muthafuckas were deaf or dumb, but they still hadn't answered the question that I had now asked three times.

"See, I told you this bitch was nuttier than trail mix. Let me spell this out for you since you can't put two and two together." TyTy clasped his hands together all extra feminine like. "The man that bought that shit and paid for your room called us in to hook you up for this boogie ass party you about to attend, ok?"

He pointed to the girl who'd introduced herself as Princess. "She's got your hair, I've got your make-up, and Lola got er'thang else." He rolled his eyes.

I looked at him and then at Princess, and my resolve softened a bit. "Well, that's all you had to say."

"Lord Jesus, give me strength. I don't need to catch a case today," TyTy mumbled.

I rolled my eyes. I was impressed with Grey's gesture, but he didn't have to hire this gay ghetto bird. Man or not, I would shoot a hot one right into his perfectly contoured face with the quickness. I pushed back thoughts of slumping his soft ass as I headed towards the door.

"I gotta run for a second and get my personal items from home. I guess ya'll can set up, and I'll be back."

The girl I now knew as Lola stepped from behind TyTy.

"Mr. Summers told me to handle anything that you need. I have his black card, so I can run out and get you anything that you may be missing." She set down the load of things in her hand and then handed me another shopping bag that was hanging from her shoulder. "Mr. Summers already purchased toiletries, a few fragrances, intimates, and an outfit for you to wear home tomorrow."

See, this man was too much. I was a rich bitch by birth, so the price tag on gifts weren't what was I was elated about. It was the fact that he'd gone out of his way to make sure that I was taken care of. That blew me away. I'd dated around a little bit, but no man had ever spoiled me like this, except for my father. Here Grey was doing this for me after a two-week long work relationship. If this nigga was trying to make me fall in love, he'd got a bitch. For real, for real.

GREY

May 2014

A nigga was swagging tonight. I was the boss so it was only right that I looked like THAT nigga. Dressed in a pair of black J Brand jeans, a black John Varvatos button down shirt, a burgundy velvet blazer courtesy of Topman and a pair of black Prada loafers, I looked like money. The gold Movado watch, five carat diamonds in my ears and the black and white silk pocket square were just something light for the haters. Although I was a street nigga, my style game was impeccable. That was the one thing my brother and I still had in common. More than pleased with my look, I headed out the door. Because I had been laying low for a while, I decided tonight was the night to go all out. I hopped into the rented Porsche 918 Spyder and made my way to the Beverly Hills hotel to pick up Nakami.

I pulled up to the Beverly Hills Hotel and Bungalows and stepped out to hand my keys to the valet. My intent was to go inside and grab Nakami, but before I could give the car to the valet attendant, she came strutting out the door.

Fuck. Me.

This woman was the epitome of beauty. Dressed in a white wrap dress with a real low v that made it impossible for her to wear a bra and neon green Giuseppe sandals, my dick got rock at the sight of her. Her toasted almond skin looked as if she'd spent all day on somebody's beach, and her super thick frame filled out every inch of the dress I'd picked out. Her curly hair was piled up on top of her head with curly strands falling down in random places.

Her smirk pulled me out of my haze. "You look incredible, *Mrs. Summers*."

She laughed at me prematurely calling her my wife. "Oh, so you tell fortunes as a side hustle?"

"Nah, I just know my future when I see it."

Nakami blushed. "You're too much. I really appreciate everything you did for me today. I'm impressed that you were able to nail my style. This is definitely something I would've picked for myself."

I walked around the car and opened the door for her and allowed her to get in the car. Then I walked to the other side and hopped into the driver's seat.

"I'm a fashion nigga," I told her. "I like to dress, and I know what I want to see my woman in."

"Oh, your woman, huh? Look at you claiming me, and you don't even know if I'm available."

"If you ain't, fuck that nigga. He lost his woman as soon as I walked in your office."

Nakami tried to hide her smile, but she was struggling. "Mr. Summers, you just don't know what you're getting yourself into."

NAKAMI

May 2014

I oozed out of the Porsche and slinked onto the red carpet that was just outside of the club, feeling like I was high on something foreign. Grey had this aura that was contagious, and being in his presence made me feel like I was untouchable. I'd planned to walk the carpet alone but Grey made his way to my side, grabbing my hand and smiling for the cameras. I couldn't help the heat I felt rising in my body as he stood close to me. I wanted to say fuck this party, take him back to the suite, and fuck him a million ways to Sunday. But I'd worked hard on this event and was anxious to experience the final product.

Grey and I finished posing for the cameras, took the elevator up to the rooftop where the club was located, and walked inside South Beach. Even over the loud music, I could hear Grey's jaw hit the floor. I had really outdone myself. You felt the undeniable presence of Miami's infamous South Beach as soon as you entered. Each booth that lined the walls was made to look like a cabana, with large, plush, white beds and white ottoman poofs. Colorful curtains outlined each booth, and flat screen TV's adorned both sides of each booth. The entire club was drenched in exotic flowers. All three bars were outfitted with Wet Willies frozen drink machines, along with every type of liquor you could imagine. My favorite part was the sand that led to the manmade beach, which was actually just a borderless infinity pool that extended to the outdoor patio. The cool blue water and white sand that led to the gorgeous view of the LA skyline made you feel like you had just been transported to the exotic location. Outside on the patio, there were more bed cabanas and large pillowy lounge chairs decorated with colorful throw pillows.

Waitresses were walking around in white pencil skirts, gold sandals, and white crop tops carrying trays of food from the menu that consisted of foods like shrimp ceviche shooters, cubano sandwich sliders, and steak and cornbread tamale bites. There were hookahs at all the VIP booths, and I had also arranged for Starbuzz Hookah to give out free hookah pens to all the attendees. DJ Mo Beatz was starting the night off bumping my favorite artist of the moment, Future, and people were starting to filter in.

"Ma, this is more dope than I could have imagined! You did your thing!"

Grey slipped his hands around my waist, pulled me close, and kissed my cheek. I was surprised and delighted at his show of affection. This nigga had no clue what the heat of his body was doing to me. And if he put his lips that close to my face again, I was bound to suck them clean off his face.

"Bay-be! You outdid yourself, bitch! This place is fucking bomb!" I knew the voice behind me immediately.

I turned around and saw my best friend, Blu, strutting over towards us. Blu Buckley, aka Blu Bucks was my bottom bitch. I'd met her my sophomore year in high school, and we'd been rocking with each other ever since. She was the definition of a down ass chick, and she was the only female I had ever really vibed with. After high school, Blu went down to ATL to get her money up by stripping in one of the hottest clubs in the country, Magic City. And she came up, let me tell you. With a body like Melyssa Ford and a face like Keyshia Dior, Blu was one of the top earners at the club. She was banking upwards of five g's a night and even more when celebrities stopped through.

After a couple years, she started missing home so I begged my dad to invest in a strip club. With a little coaxing, he agreed and I brought Blu home to manage the place. She still did one night only's every month, but she was the boss lady now and doing a damn good job making sure our strip club was the most exclusive in the city. I supported her, and she always had my back.

I ran up to Blu and hugged her. She was dressed in a beige Herve Leger bandage dress and a pair of coral Yves Saint Laurent peep toe sandals. Her shoulder length blue bob was bone straight with a side swept bang, and I didn't miss the large

Stuart Weitzman hoops dangling from her ears. My bitch was bad.

Blu pulled away from our hug and scoped out Grey over my shoulder. "Damn, daddy. Who the fuck is that? I need his number like yesterday!"

"Blu, you better back down, bitch. That's my nigga now."

"You got it, boss! But since when you get a man?"

"Since today, nosy. This is his club. He came through my office last week and asked me to make his place the new hot spot. Then he proceeded to woo me with Michael Costello, a personal hair and make-up team, and the Presidential Bungalow Suite at the Beverly Hills Hotel."

"Damn! After two weeks? Shit, he got a brother?" Blu joked.

Grey swaggered up to us. "Actually I do. Ladies, this is my brother Kimani. Kimani this is Nakami, the party planner and my lady, and her friend..."

Blu's eyes lit up at the sight of Kimani. She extended her hand to him. "Blu. Blu Buckley."

Kimani and Grey's parents had to have both been models, because Kimani definitely hadn't missed out on the beauty gene. Standing about 6'3" with smooth butterscotch skin, light green eyes, and slick dark hair, Kimani reminded me a lot of Don Benjamin from America's Next Top Model. Unconsciously, he licked his lips as he looked Blu up and down.

He was dressed in a pair of white jeans, white button down, and cobalt blue blazer. I recognized the Gucci loafers on his feet and the Rolex watch on his wrist, so I knew his pockets had to be heavy. I winked at Blu, signaling my approval of Kimani.

"Nice to meet you both." He smiled revealing perfectly straight white teeth and one dimple in his left cheek.

"Mmph, I've seen you before," Blue told him. "Do you come to Clappers often or something?"

"That strip club in Hollywood?" he asked her. "Nah, ma. I heard it be popping though." He looked Blu over again. "You got the body for it, but I wouldn't believe it if you told me you were a dancer."

"Well, seeing is believing, boo. Don't let the corporate face fool you. I was the ass that started the twerk movement. But I'm the general manager there now." Blu frowned her face up and began circling Kimani like an animal surveying its prey. "This is going to bother me all night." Blu walked up on him, getting real close to his face. Grabbing his face with her hand and turning it to the side, she looked at the collage of tattoos that were on his neck and she smiled. "You're a model. That's where I've seen you."

"You remembered my tattoo?"

"No, I remembered that big ass bulge in them Calvin Klein's you were advertising. I just wanted a reason to touch you."

Kimani grinned. "The way you stretching out the fabric of that dress with all that ass and hips, not to mention ya cute ass face, baby girl you don't need a reason to get close to me." Kimani wrapped his hands around Blu's waist and pulled her close to his body without breaking eye contact.

"Ya'll wild!" Grey laughed at his brother and Blu. It looked like the night was off to a great start.

GREY

May 2014

Nakami had put on for a nigga. The club was slapping! She had celebrities coming in and out, the music was live, and to top it off I was walking around with the baddest bitch in the state. Press was there snapping pictures and taking video of red carpet arrivals, and all the gossip sites from Bossip to Necole Bitchie to Baller Alert were in the building. I knew that South Beach was already well on its way to becoming the newest spot to party in LA. Nakami and I had settled into a secluded booth in the corner of the club where the waitress had brought us our passion fruit hookah. We were enjoying each other's company when two tall, muscular men appeared at our booth. I reached for the gun I carry in my waistband, but Nakami gently placed her hand over mine.

I recognized the man that appeared from behind the bodyguards because he was a legend. Dressed in a clean black, Gucci tuxedo, an untied bow tie, and Salvatore Ferragamo dress shoes, he exuded power and his presence demanded everyone's respect. His skin tone was dark for his Japanese heritage, and his jet black hair with a thick streak of gray was slicked back with what looked like an entire tub of gel. To be honest, he looked just like one of the boss niggas from Rush Hour 2. The long scar that started at the top of his left eyebrow and ended at the bottom of his chin was the only thing that made him recognizable to me. Not that I'd ever seen this man in person a day in my life, but he was a legend whose stories were the things hood fairytales were made of. This nigga was epic. But what confused me was why he was here. I didn't know the nigga and, from what I'd heard, he didn't really make many public appearances. A confused expression blanketed my face as I wracked my brain trying to figure out why he was at my shit. I didn't even notice that Nakami had left my side until I saw her rushing the dude in front of me.

"Daughter, you've done a beautiful job!" He congratulated her and wrapped her in his arms.

Daughter? Nakami was Hero Yukimura's daughter? The chick whose back I was preparing to break after the party was over was the daughter of one of the most legendary drug lords of my time? I wanted to get up and hit my dougie, do the Nae Nae, do a praise dance, or something! Not only was the chick on my arm bad, but her family was the plug I needed to get back on top. I had come up on a gold mine, and I didn't even know it. I had to play my cards right, because a hook up this proper could get me straight for life.

"Thank you, daddy. Daddy, I want to introduce you to the owner and my client." Nakami smiled at me sweetly as she pulled her father by the hand. I stood up to greet him.

"Dad, this is Grey Summers, the owner of this club. Grey, this is my father, Hero Yukimura."

I extended my hand to Hero, and we shook. His facial expression remained like stone as he gave me a once over.

"What do you do for a living, Grey? How can you afford to rehab a club and pay my daughter's exorbitant party planning prices?" He smirked slightly at his last statement. Nakami playfully hit him in the arm.

"I'm in the trade business. Unfortunately, business has slowed due to relocation," I stated, hoping that he caught my drift.

He remained silent for a moment, and then he nodded his head. "Is that right? Are you interested in my daughter?"

"Absolutely," I said without hesitation.

"You're a strong presence, Grey. I too am in the trade business and may be able to help you get situated. Here is my business card. Call me Monday to set up a meeting."

He pulled a card from his back pocket and handed it to me. I almost grabbed his ass and hugged him. I was too geeked. Although I had been peeping the scene for four months, as soon as I had set my sights on making my presence known on the streets things seemed to be falling into place with little effort. I wasn't always the biggest fan of organized religion or church, but someone up there had to be looking out for a nigga, for real.

"I appreciate it, Mr. Yukimura."

"Call me Hero. As long as you keep my daughter happy, your life will be easy. Fuck up and…well…I can promise you won't live long enough to regret it."

I couldn't argue or be mad at his threat. She was his daughter and, as desperately as I needed this plug, I wouldn't do anything to jeopardize it. I would treat his daughter like the fucking Queen of England if need be.

"I understand."

"Now I will leave you to finish celebrating," Hero told me. "I wish you success on your club, Grey."

"Thank you." We shook hands again, and then Hero hugged Nakami tightly and placed a kiss on her forehead. He departed with his security behind him.

I turned to Nakami. I looked at her differently now. She wasn't just the fine ass party planner with the fiery personality and coke bottle body. She was now my meal ticket, my lucky charm, my money bag. Just the thought of the money that could come from linking up with her dad made my dick rise against my dress pants. Adjusting myself, I pulled Nakami close to me, breathing in a mixture of her fruity body wash and her spicy perfume. Without speaking another word, I placed my lips against hers. Her body loosened against mine, as she got lost in the kiss.

When I finally pulled away, Nakami's eyes stayed closed and she smiled a dream-like smile. "He likes you, you know?"

"Yeah?"

"He doesn't do business with people off rip like that. There is something about you, Grey." She smiled wickedly before she grabbed my hand, led me back to the cabana style booth, and closed the curtains.

NAKAMI

June 2014

"Tristan, please don't forget to email the Sutter's about their wine list. We need that finalized before the end of the week." I called out.

Tristan poked her head in my office and smiled. "You got it, boss. I'm having Kelsey and Leighton pick up the flowers for tomorrow's event in the morning, and I'll meet them at the venue before seven."

"Sounds good! Well, I'm about to finalize the board for that fundraiser pitch, and then I'm going to head out. Can you start organizing the textiles for the Marco wedding?" I stood from my chair and started to gather the things I needed for the concept board. I thought Tristan had left from the doorway until she spoke again.

"You know, whatever Grey is doing to you...it' working." She leaned against the wall with her arms folded across her chest.

"Excuse me?"

"I mean you've been so much more laid back since he's been in your life. You're calmer and more patient. I like this new you. He must be putting it down, girl!"

Oh hell no! Now I could agree that Grey's presence had brought about a calmer, more Zen version of myself, but this little bitch here had some nerve. I was her boss, not her bff. Who was dipping in and out of my honeypot was none of her concern. Her even opening her mouth to comment just pissed me off. If she wanted me to bring the bitch, back she had just pressed the right buttons to resurrect her.

"It's a shame that I have to remind you of this because I am sure that I haven't give you any indication otherwise, but our relationship is a professional one. You are not my friend. You are my employee. I don't care what you do outside of these four walls and you shouldn't care what I do either," I spoke. "Regardless of what or who is responsible for my recent change, we will not be bonding about it over Caesar salad and white wine spritzers like two fucking sorority sisters. Mind your business, do your job and keep your commentary to yourself. Got it?"

Tristan nodded her head and quickly exited my office. The fuck? I just know this broad didn't think that I liked her because I had dialed back the bitch lately. See, Grey had me fucking up. Got me out here making chicks feel comfortable and shit. I could feel myself letting my guard down. This man was making me so happy that I had fucked around and let people think I was nice. Since Grey and I had started seeing each other, I had been on cloud nine and it had been hard for me to switch from doting girlfriend to Devil Wears Prada when I got to work. Now I had messed around and made a friend. I needed to get it together. Thoughts of Grey and I's earlier steamy text message exchange swirled around my head, causing me to break out in a wide grin. With Grey on my mind, I took out my phone to send him a quick text message.

June 17, 1:58 PM Me: Hey, boo. You want to grab dinner at Toca Madera's tonight?

Knowing that he was probably busy, I set the phone down on my desk and went to work. A good hour later, I had the concept board halfway finished and decided to take a break. The first thing I did was check my phone to see if Grey had replied back. He hadn't. I felt the tips of my ears turn hot before I started pacing the floor.

I knew he could be busy with the club, but what the fuck else could he be doing that he wasn't able to answer a quick text within an hour? I mean, it only takes a few seconds to answer yes or no, right? Just a few key strokes was all it took! The more I thought about it, the angrier I became. If there was one thing that I hated to be, it was ignored.

Grey was usually great at responding to me and picking up when I called, but I had started to notice he had begun to be a little more lax than usual. I hadn't paid much attention to it, but he definitely had my attention now. My thing was that he couldn't be that busy at the club. It was 3:30 pm on a

Wednesday! He didn't have a party until tomorrow! What the hell was he doing, huh? I could feel the irritation turning to anger, so I decided to try again before I lost my cool. Quickly, I sent another text.

June 17, 3:06PM Me: You know I have to make a reservation if you want to go. Let me know ASAP.

I stared at my phone as I continued to pace the floor. This nigga better answer me. The fuck could he be doing? He better not be with another bitch! I saw the way them little plastic model hoes that worked at the club looked at him. Let me find out that one of those little thirst buckets were slanging their box his way! I'm going to---

Ding!

The notification on my phone stopped my rant midsentence. I swiped my thumb across the screen and clicked on my messages with a smile slowing creeping across my face. It faded when I realized it was just Blu.

June 17, 3:08PM Blu: Hey girl. I need your help. Meet me on Rodeo?

Shit, Blu! Now was not the time! I clicked ignore and went back to pacing the floor. Why wasn't he answering me? See, I hated when men did this. One simple little response could kill all the doubt swimming around in my brain. But no, instead of replying no matter how simple the answer, a nigga will leave you hanging all damn day, making you think of every possible scenario that could be causing you to get ignored.

My mind ran a million miles a minute as I went down the list of reasons why he hadn't responded to me. *He could just be busy, right? Or...he could be face deep in another bitch's pussy! Calm down, he could be driving!* I thought to myself. *He hates to text and drive. Or...he could be giving one of them bottle models he hired the long stroke on top of his desk!*

"Ughhhh!" I screamed. This was driving me nuts!

"You good, ma?" a deep voice rumbled.

I whipped around so fast that I almost fell over. Leaning against the door frame was Grey dressed in pair of camo shorts, a snug white tee underneath a crisp blue jean shirt, a navy blue Detroit snapback and some Jordan 3's. My heart rate sped up at the sight of my fine ass man. His presence immediately caused my irritation to dissipate.

Gathering myself quickly, I smiled at him. "Grey, what are you doing here?"

Instead of answering, he closed the door behind him and smirked.

"Grey..." I looked at him curiously.

He walked over to me slowly, licking his lips and coming out of his jean shirt without taking his sultry, grey eyes off of me. In one swift move, he had ripped my Stella McCartney skirt from its middle seam, hoisted me up by my waist and wrapped my legs around him. I gasped as chills shot up my spine and my panties moistened. Grey kissed me roughly and I replied with an intense kiss of my own. All semblance of anger had vanished and now I just wanted him to fuck me into oblivion. I was horny beyond words.

I hurriedly pulled his t-shirt over his head before he ripped open the front of my blouse, sending buttons flying everywhere. He didn't bother unhooking my bra; he just freed my D-cups from their lace prison and pulled them into his mouth. I squealed as his teeth grazed my erect nipples. His warm, wet mouth was causing tremors to shoot through the nerve endings in my breasts, eliciting a shudder from my body. I tossed my head back and arched my back, allowing him better access. With my breasts still in his mouth, Grey used his index and middle finger to move my thongs to the side and plunge inside of me. Instinctively, I clenched my muscles, wrapped my walls around his fingers and pulled him in deeper. I pushed both of my large breasts together and edged them towards his mouth. He responded to my suggestive gesture by biting down lightly on my nipples that now resembled two Hershey kisses, and a low moan tumbled from my lips.

"You wet as fuck, ma," he growled into my ear.

Something about the way that he talked to me with that Midwest twang made my clit jump every time. Briefly, I let my eyes travel down, wanting to see Grey in action, and met his gaze. A wicked smiled crossed his lips as he used his index and middle finger to stir my juices and his thumb to stroke my love button. Without breaking his rhythm, Grey crossed the room and laid me down on the leather sectional. I let my eyes roam his perfectly chiseled body that was covered in beautiful tattoos and couldn't help but think about how fucking lucky I was. My thoughts were interrupted when Grey hooked one finger into the middle of my soaked Dita Von Teese lace thongs, and eased down my body until his face was eye level with my pussy. My breath caught when he gripped my thighs and pulled me closer to his face; I was eagerly anticipating the tongue lashing he was preparing to give me.

Nothing happened for the next few moments. I was hot and wet and this nigga wanted to just sit there with my pussy in his face. I waited in agony for his lips, tongue or his fingers to touch me, but all I could feel was his breath tickling my clit, teasing me with the thought of what was to come. Sick of his shit, I pushed his head right where I needed him to go and wrapped my legs around his neck, making sure he wasn't going anywhere anytime soon. I heard him chuckle, but I didn't see a damn thing funny as I almost choked on my own spit when his stiff tongue finally made contact with my swollen pearl.

"Mmmm..." I gripped the couch cushions and squirmed against the hot leather fabric as I felt his tongue do laps around my clit. He gave me long, slow strokes at first, like he was eating chocolate soft serve. And best believe I was melting right into his mouth and my juices were spilling all over his thick, expertly skilled tongue. I moved my hips in rhythm with his tongue stroke and I felt small shots of electricity shoot from my toes up my spine.

"Oh God!" I suddenly screamed.

This nigga had the audacity to let his tongue vibrate against my clit. That shit had my ass ready to wave a white flag! I swear his tongue was battery operated because no man's tongue could move at that speed without some assistance. He had me out of breath and I wasn't even doing shit! I started backing away from him, scared that I was about to experience some shit I wasn't ready for, but Grey wasn't having that.

"Bring that ass back here," he grumbled while latching on to my hips and bringing my body back towards his face. "You wanted that shit, so you gon' take it."

I couldn't fight his strong ass if I wanted to. He pulled my clit back into his mouth and sucked on it like a watermelon Jolly Rancher. I grabbed a handful of his dreads and moaned so loud that I was surprised Tristan didn't come running her nosey ass to the door to see what was wrong. He continued to give me a tongue lashing that felt so good and tortured me so bad that it felt like punishment. I was running from him like I stole something, but I probably would have swung on him if he had attempted to stop. Mixed emotions flowed through me as I welcomed the feeling his was giving me and rejected it all at the same time. It was too much.

"Fuckkkkk Grey, shit!"

Grey's tongue swirled around my clit. Then he dipped it right inside me and fucked me with his tongue like it was the thick rod hanging between his legs. I swallowed hard as he took his finger and massaged my clit while still darting his tongue in and out of me. I lost my damn mind. An orgasm came sweeping through my body, making me feel lightheaded as hell. My juices came pouring out like rain and Grey was there to collect every drop with his tongue. Two tears escaped from my eyes; his head game was just that vicious. Grey stood up and laughed before he took a few tissues from the box on my desk, wiped his mouth and laughed again.

"Your lil' feisty ass was about to go ham on a nigga, wasn't you?" He grinned as he reached for his shirt.

"What?" I said barely above a whisper. I was still stuck off the orgasm Grey had just gave me.

"When I ain't answer. If I didn't come when I did, your crazy ass would have come looking for me." He laughed again. "No fucking chill."

I propped myself up on my elbows and looked at him as he placed his snapback on his head and attempted to walk towards the door.

"The fuck you goin'?" I asked with attitude. I know this nigga didn't think he was about to leave.

"To the club. I got a meeting in an hour. Don't worry, I'ma handle that tonight." He threw a smile my way and turned back towards the door.

Aw, hell naw! This nigga got me all fucked up. His smooth ass thought that he was just going to waltz in my job, interrupt my meeting, get me all worked up and dip? Naw, he must not know who he's fucking with. Before Grey could reach the door, I hopped up off the couch and shoved the office chair past him and towards the door, blocking his exit.

"Nakami, for real. I gotta get back to work."

"Fuck work, nigga."

I pushed him down onto the chair and went to work unbuckling his pants. He made a weak ass attempt to brush my hands away, but that nigga knew he wanted to fuck me as bad as I wanted to fuck him. I got his shorts undone in no time and pulled out his long, thick pretty ass dick. It was already hard for me, so I stroked it a few times before I hopped right on. I took a seat on his lap and used my hand to guide him inside of me.

"Shit…" Grey moaned.

I smirked because now it was my turn to pay that ass back. If he thought he was the only one with some tricks up his sleeve, he thought wrong. I started off slow, planting my feet on the ground and pushing off to get a good bounce going. I made sure to squeeze my muscles around his dick before I came all the way down. Multi-tasking, I licked and sucked on his neck, making sure I left a hickey on his light bright ass. He smacked my ass hard and I grinned to myself. I sped up my rhythm, leaned into Grey's body and bounced my ass instead of using my entire body. I built a steady rhythm to the beat in my head and could feel the tip of his dick hitting my spot. I let off a moan as I felt another orgasm building up.

Grey pulled on my long, wavy hair. "Ride that shit, ma."

Oh, I was going to ride it alright. Changing it up, I started to wind my hips in a circular motion, rolling my body like I was full-blooded Jamaican. I could sense Grey losing control of his body by the way his eyes were rolling in the back of his head. Oh no, he wasn't going to get off that easy. Forcing my breast in his face, I leaned back and hooked my heels into the bottom of the chair and rode him like a mechanical bull. I lassoed his dick with my slippery walls and twisted my hips so that he could hit every corner, pocket, crook and crevice.

"Gottdamn, you got some good pussy, girl. Shit."

I heard his toes crack and I had to stifle a giggle. He gripped my ass and dug his nails into my cheeks as he tried to hold his nut off. Naw, he was going to give me that nut. Slowly I rose from his lap so that only the tip of his dick was inside and just waited. His eyes popped open when he felt me stop moving.

"What the fuck, Naka-"

Before he could finish his sentence, I clenched my walls around him and slammed my body onto his lap.

"SHIT!" he yelled out.

I rose up again and waited. He bit down on his lip so hard I thought he was going to draw blood. He tried to slam me back down but I held firm. When I was ready, I clenched my muscles, gripping his dick inside me, and slowly slid back down, twisting my hips again before I landed back on his lap. He sucked his lip in, trying not to scream like a little bitch, and I laughed out loud. This time I rose but when I slid back down, I popped my ass and brought my lower body forward in a scooping motion, so that my clit rubbed up against him. The sensation drove me wild. I was nearing my peak, but I wanted to make him come at the same time. I picked up speed and bounced all over his member. He had my shit good and gushy because the only noise that could be heard in the room was the sound of my overflow of juices being stirred. Grey started matching my rhythm and fucking me back.

"Mhmmm…" we said in unison.

I did my signature "stand and slam" move once more before Grey said, "Fuck this," and he picked my ass up.

"You think I'm bout to let you fuck me?" he whispered before he thrust himself into me hard, still holding my body up in the air. My smile quickly faded when he started fucking me at a pace that made me dizzy. He reached up and grabbed the back of my head, forcing my lips to his and kissed me roughly. I bit down on his lip and dug my nails into his back. Grey now had me laying across my desk, flat on my back with one hand on my shoulder and the other hand on my hip, driving into me like he was trying to break something. I grabbed up my titties in my hand and pinched my nipples, heightening the sensation of the orgasm that was beginning to break.

"Grey... I'm cum---"

Before I could get the sentence all the way out my mouth, Grey pulled out. He wiped the film of sweat that formed on his forehead with the back of his hand and looked at my agape mouth in amusement.

"Nigga, you can't be serious!" I screamed.

"You the one that want to play games," he chuckled.

I laughed to myself. Grey was going to learn today. He was riding with a true freak, and if he thought that I was going to sit up here and play games with him when he was the one that bust up in my office trying to get nasty, he had another thing coming. Without taking my eyes off him, I spread my legs wide and planted my gold Giuseppe sandals up on the desk and eased my hand down my stomach, over my freshly waxed pussy and inserted two fingers into the spot he'd just left. I used my thumb to play with my clit and my other hand to pinch at my nipples. Moans echoed off the wall and my eyes slammed shut. I continued my show and it felt so good that I didn't give a fuck if Grey finished or not; I was getting mine regardless. Suddenly, I felt my hand being moved and replaced by Grey's hard tool and I smirked.

"You a stone cold freak, girl. Fuck." He smiled at me and I smiled back.

He continued to deliver long stroke after long stroke until we both came one after the other. Grey landed on top of me, and I looked up at the ceiling trying to catch my breath. My eyes fluttered open after a few moments, and I swore I saw emoji hearts floating above my head. This man was incredible. Just when I thought I was going to have to show my ass, Grey popped up and gave me a dose of act right. He was the yin to my yang, and the calm to my storm. I was beginning to think that Grey and I were perfect for each other. I knew it was early on in the "relationship" or whatever this was, but I was already envisioning a beach wedding, 2.5 kids and a house in the hills. I loved living as a single, independent career woman, but I would be lying if I said I wouldn't give that up to have a man like Grey be my husband. And if I played my cards right, he would belong to me soon enough.

GREY

July 2014

"So what would my schedule look like?" Niema asked me. She crossed her legs seductively, leaned forward and propped her arms up on her knee. Her new position gave me a better view of her nice sized titties that were threatening to tumble out of her low cut shirt. I swallowed hard.

Interviewing these dancers for the club was becoming harder and harder every day. They were coming dressed in less and less clothing and I couldn't front; most of these chicks were Smooth Magazine fine. It had been a couple Draya's, a few K. Michelle's, a handful of Amber Rose's and a bad ass chick that was the thicker version of Ciara and she could move like her too. I was having a hard time focusing on being professional and had thought about letting Kimani and my club manager, Trickie, come in and do the interviews for me. Kimani was out in New York for some kind of photo shoot and I had Trickie doing inventory, so that was a no-go.

I was really feeling Nakami, and we had recently decided to make things official, but I couldn't deny the fact that I had pussy being thrown at me left and right since I'd opened the club. Half the chicks I had interviewed in the last day and a half had been tossing the draws at me non-stop. It was getting more difficult to shrug off the temptation. It had been a grip since I'd had another chick, but I was going to try my hand at being a one woman nigga.

"You would be working the hours of the club which would be Thursday thru Sunday from 9pm to 2am. Of course if we have special events during the days we aren't normally operational, you would be required to come in on those days as well," I spoke. The entire time I spoke, Niema had her tongue gliding across her glossy lips and I could barely concentrate.

"Ok, that's cool," Niema smiled.

"Cool. So did you have something prepared to show me?"

"Yup. I gave the Dj my music already."

I signaled for the DJ to turn on her track and a few seconds later, The Weekend's *Often* came blaring through the speakers. Niema shook off her jean jacket, stood from the couch and ran her hands up the side of her body. I leaned back in the cabana style booth and watched as she wound her thick and toned body to the beat. She was an okay dancer; she mostly snaked her hips or ran her hands through her shoulder length blonde hair, but she had mad sex appeal. She never broke eye contact and she caressed herself to the point where I was unsure if she was dancing or if she was in the middle of foreplay. I was so caught up in watching Niema that I didn't know anyone had entered the room until the song stopped. I looked up and saw Nakami marching over to us from the DJ booth. Fuck!

"Why did the music stop?" Niema looked at me with an eyebrow raised.

"Niema, I'm going to give you a call…"

"No, the fuck he ain't. You can take ya Baby Gap jacket and Ross heels and carry your ass out my man's face!" Nakami flung Niema's jacket in her face, almost knocking the girl over.

This shit was starting to become a problem. Nakami and I had been dating for almost two months. I swear I might have even been falling for her. Everything was cool right up until business at the club started picking up and I started spending a little more time at work. Nakami started with little snide comments about spending more time at work than with her, and then it escalated to her doing drive-bys and pop ups. I'm not the type of nigga to hide shit because I ain't ever felt the need to lie about what I do as a grown ass man, so I had told her all about the interviews last week. That's when shit really got out of hand.

At first, she tried to make it seem like she wanted to help vet the girls. She claimed that she used to help Blu run Clappers when it first opened and she had an eye for talent. I quickly found out that her lil' jealous ass just wanted to be nosey. The first day of interviews I had a list of ten girls that were supposed to come through the club. I looked up and it was 1 o'clock, but not one of them had showed up. I ended up calling the next interviewee and found out that she had received a call from a woman stating that the interviews had been cancelled until further notice. What type of shit was that, man? I was 38 hot!

But I had to play it cool. Nakami's father had been out of town for the last month or so, so I still hadn't been able to kick it about getting back on. I was feeling Nakami, no doubt, but she was starting to show signs of a crazy bitch and I wasn't ready for those type of problems.

"Yo! What the hell is your problem?" I pulled Nakami to the side and raised my finger, asking Niema to give me a second.

"I know you not out here fucking Kmart ass hoes now?" she shouted as she eyeballed Neima.

"No. I'm interviewing dancers for the club, like I told your ass I would be! What reason do I have to lie to you?" I asked.

"Every reason, nigga! I looked through your phone this morning and a bitch named---"

I cut her off. "You went through my phone?!" I yelled.

She had definitely crossed the line. I could feel myself ready to fuck some shit up, and if Nakami didn't get out my face soon, she was liable to become collateral damage.

"It was ringing incessantly this morning!"

"Fuck that, Nakami. You don't pay my fucking bill. Stay off my shit and I'm for real," I said seriously. "Secondly, I'm at work. I don't have time to be arguing with you about some frivolous shit that you can't seem to understand. I'm interviewing. That's it. I'm not explaining this shit to you again."

Nakami looked at me with fire burning behind her eyes. I knew that even if she left right now, this wouldn't be the end of this conversation. And I was going to have to put her in her place gently because I still needed her to set things up with her father. I couldn't mess that shit up.

"You know what Grey? Fuck you!" she pushed me in my chest and ran out of the front door of the club.

I pinched the bridge of my nose and took a deep breath. I walked over to Niema, who was still standing there trying to process the scene she had just witnessed.

"Look, I'm sorry about that."

"No worries, boo. Trust me, I've seen worse. We gon' finish this interview or nah?" She grinned.

I smiled back at her, knowing that after that comment, she already had the job. If she could handle Nakami, she could handle anything she might encounter at the club. Now the question was, could I handle Nakami and for how fucking long?

BLU

July 2014

I stood in front of the mirror, a nervous wreck; *me*, Blu Buckley, the bitch who used to twerk sum'n for a few bills, the chick that used to get on a stage surrounded by drunk and horny men and fulfill every single one of their fantasies, the broad that never gave a fuck was about to go on a date and I was sweating bullets like I was testifying in open court.

Something about Kimani scared the shit out of me. After our initial encounter at Grey's grand opening, we'd exchanged phone numbers and kicked it via text and FaceTime. He was observant, smooth, aggressive, and confident bordering on cocky. He had this sexual aura that bled through the phone, and I couldn't count how many times I felt my grown ass blushing after the things he said. He was refreshing, sexy and mad cool.

So why was I nervous? Because this nigga seemed too good to be true, and I could definitely see myself falling for him. And that was a big no-no in my book. I had done the relationship thing a time or two, but most niggas thought my job defined me as a person. Because I was a stripper I was expected to be their personal sex slave, their blow-up doll, their 24/7 fantasy. But fuck that! I was a person too! I wanted to be wined, dined and made love to. I grew tired of the constant fucking and late night chill sessions.

Besides the fact that niggas never thought I was good enough for more than a quick nut, I never believed that I was worth more than that either. So once I realized that I deserved better, I sought out better. Or so I thought. Enter Ronelle Kurt. Standing 5'11" with skin the color of a Hershey's bar and smooth dark hair, I thought Ronelle was it. I loved that man to the edge of the earth and back. That was until I found out the nigga was married with a kid on the way. My dumb ass didn't take the lack of public outings and the consistent late night rendezvous as signs that something wasn't right with our relationship before it was too late.

I'd always talked shit about the girls who acted like the earth was ending when their nigga broke up with them, but I finally understood their pain. It was excruciating and unlike anything I'd ever felt before. So I said fuck love and changed my mentality back to being focused on the money. Now the fact that love, feelings and dates were things that were all back on the table terrified me. I was terrified of the set-up and the letdown that was bound to happen. But on the other hand, me and my money were getting lonely. I just wasn't sure if I was ready to get back in the saddle yet. Kimani was a hard man to resist and, because he had been so insistent on taking me out, I finally caved and we set a date. Now the day was here, and I wanted to throw up the fear that was bubbling in my stomach.

"Miss Buckley, you have a guest in the lobby named Mr. Kimani Summers. Would you like me to send him up?" The doorman's voice boomed through the intercom system.

I walked over to the speaker and pressed a button to speak. "No, tell him I'll be right down."

I took a deep breath, grabbed my phone from its charger, and exited my luxury pad. I took the elevator down and used the time to check my reflection again to make sure everything was on point.

Dressed in a pair of skin tight white jeans by AG Jeans, a white knit turtleneck crop top with no bra, and a peach colored leather motorcycle jacket by Rebecca Minkoff, I looked fresh and flirty. The white open-toe fringe sandals by Charline De Luca added "umph" to my outfit, and my long blue extensions were pulled up in a high ponytail with a few loose pieces pulled down to frame my face. I had to admit that I looked stunning and cool, without looking like I was trying too hard.

Butterflies fluttered around my stomach as the elevator began to slow. 6, 5, 4, 3, 2, G... I took another deep breath and stepped off the elevator. I smiled wide at the sight of Kimani holding a large bouquet of purple orchids. He smiled that sexy ass grin when he saw me, and my panties got wet right on cue.

"Hey, beautiful." His voice was raspy and deep; it was a tone that made you want to close your eyes and wish that he was using it to whisper sweet nothings right in your ear.

"Hi," I said shyly. I walked up on him, taking the flowers from his hand and giving him a church hug. He was *not* with that. Kimani grabbed me by my waist firmly and pulled my body into his. I could feel his lips lingering near my ear, and I swear I turned to putty right there.

"Don't try and play me like I'm that ugly nigga with no game that's always pressing you for a hug. Give a real nigga a real hug, girl," he whispered.

I blushed so hard that I thought I had permanently changed skin tones. I wrapped my arms around him, giving him the real hug that he requested. His hands roaming my ass didn't go unnoticed, but I didn't say anything about it.

"Thank you for the flowers."

"No doubt. You ready to go?"

"Yeah, one second." I walked over to the concierge desk. "Brent, could you take these up to my place, put them in some water, and set them on the foyer table? There should be some vases underneath the kitchen sink." I handed him the bouquet.

"No problem, Miss. Buckley. Have a good night."

Kimani and I walked out of my apartment building and approached his Range. He opened the door for me, and I slid in while he walked around and hopped in on his side. We pulled off with some Miguel playing on low and the sunroof open displaying the starry sky.

Kimani glanced over at me and smiled.

"What?" I asked, starting to feel shy again under his gaze.

"Why you seem so nervous? You were bold as fuck when we met at my brother's party, and now you're all quiet."

I giggled. "You're going to laugh if I tell you the real reason."

"Try me."

"I've never been on a real date."

He was quiet. A perplexed look fell over his face and when he could afford to take his eyes off the road to look at me, he did. "What you mean you've never been on a real date?"

"I've never been. Like when a dude picks me up, takes me to do shit, pays for it, and takes me to the crib. I've never been on a date." Having to break it down like that was embarrassing.

"Why not?" he asked.

I opened my mouth to speak, but what was I going to say? That I was a reformed hoe who no one respected enough to ask out on a real date? That I was better known as a one-hitter-quitter in most niggas books? The fact that I had already admitted that I'd never been taken out was embarrassing enough.

"You know what? It don't even matter. You're going to have your first official date tonight, and I'll make it one you won't forget." He winked at me.

Surprised but elated that he didn't further press the issue, I smiled and relaxed against the soft peanut butter colored leather seats.

****

"Kimani! What are we doing? We can't go in here. It's closed!" I looked at him like he had fucking lost it when he dragged me to the entrance of the Santa Monica Pier. It was damn near midnight, and I just knew this nigga wasn't about to have me doing no illegal shit.

The date had been hella bomb so far. He'd taken me to Mastro's in Beverly Hills, and their food was delish. After dinner, we roamed around Beverly Hills until we found a bar we liked and stopped in to talk and grab some drinks.

I'd learned a lot about Kimani, and I was definitely impressed. He'd told me all about his life growing up with Grey in Detroit and the death of his girlfriend that lead him to California. He'd put in a lot of work to make it in the modeling world—taking gigs with little known designers, building his portfolio, and doing practically taking anything he could just so that he could get the attention of a modeling agency. When he signed on with Stephanie Diego, she'd told him that his charm and personality would get him more than a few print and runway gigs. Now he was pursuing a career in acting. I found myself feeling proud of this man that I had just met. We were a lot alike, and I was really enjoying his company.

"Girl, stop being such a damn scaredy cat," he laughed.

A few moments later, a man walked up to the gate, unlocked the padlock, and ushered us in. Confused, I stepped past the gate and instantly the whole pier lit up. Kimani took my hand and led me to the cotton candy stand, where there was a man standing behind the counter.

"What is all this?" I asked.

"When you said that you had never been on a date before, I knew I had to make this shit live. I know some people that know some people that like making a little money on the side, so they let us come to enjoy the pier after hours." He laughed and I joined him. "But seriously, I can't understand why the niggas you've messed with before never noticed how special you are and how deserving you are of something dope."

I blushed even harder than before. This man was something else.

"So, we got this whole thing to ourselves. What you wanna do first?" he smirked.

I stood there speechless. I was blown away that, after only knowing me for a short amount of time, he cared enough to try and make an impression. I didn't understand what I had done to deserve someone like him, but I sent a quick one up to God saying thank you. My only fear was that I would let the anxiety inside me stifle what this could grow into. Knowing me and my cold heart, I would end up ruining this before it got started good. But tonight, I would just go with it.

NAKAMI

July 2014

I walked onto the porch and used one of my ornately decorated stiletto nails to press the doorbell. I watched as the maid came flying into the foyer, walked up, and opened the large wrought-iron doors.

"Good Afternoon, Ms. Yokimura. Your father is waiting for you on the patio." Phylicia smiled widely and greeted me with open arms. I embraced her and stepped back to introduce her to Grey.

"Phylicia, this is my boyfriend, Kendrick Summers, but you can call him Grey. Grey, this is Phylicia, my old nanny and my dad's housekeeper."

Grey smiled and extended his hand for her to shake. She ignored his hand and pulled him into her wide and ample bosom, smothering him with affection.

"You're such a beautiful man. You all will have such pretty babies!" she exclaimed.

"I sure hope to have a house full of them," I laughed as I turned to Grey. The grimace that flashed on his face didn't go unnoticed.

He recovered well; smiling and ignoring her comment. "It's a pleasure to meet you."

"Well c'mon here. You know Hero is not a patient man."
She waved at us to follow her. We walked through the spacious
new home that my father had recently purchased and trailed
Phylicia to the patio area. Laid in expensive stone and
overlooking a deep blue infinity pool, the patio was gorgeous.
It was a perfect summer day out, and my father had hired a chef
to cater lunch for this meeting with Grey. I was excited for them
to sit down and talk. I stepped outside, the light wind picking
up the hem of my off white ABS fit and flare dress. My father's
eyes lit up at the sight of me.

"Daughter. It's so good to see you." He reached out for a
hug and held me close. I inhaled the scent of his Acqua De
Parma cologne and smiled. He pulled away from me and
greeted Grey.

"Grey, it's nice to see you again." The men shook hands,
and Grey mirrored my father's sentiments. "Come. I've had the
chef prepare us a wonderful meal."

We joined my father at the large outdoor table that was
decorated like Martha Stewart was his hired help. There was
food everywhere. My father had the chef made my favorite
Japanese dish, Takoyoki, which is basically fried octopus
smothered in Takoyaki sauce and Japanese mayo, and topped
with a sprinkle of dried green seaweed and katsuobushi. There
was also plenty of sushi, shrimp and chicken stir-fry, rice, and
steamed vegetables. I hadn't had a home-cooked Japanese meal

in a while, so I was quick to dive in while Grey and my father preferred to talk a little business.

"So, Grey, I have inquired about you. I understand that your well has dried up since your connect was busted. Was that what prompted your move to LA?"

"Yes. I tried a few more avenues while at home, but none of the product was worth the money they were asking for it. My old plug was the truth and if I can't get the same or better product, it wouldn't be worth my time."

I shoveled a forkful of food into my mouth as I watched them talk. Their conversation faded, as my thoughts became louder and louder. Grey was the most amazing man I'd ever met. Sure, we'd only met a few months ago but he was my future, and couldn't anyone tell me any different. Let me just run down the list of reasons why I was falling in love with this man and quickly.

For one, he was gorgeous and he matched my fly. He already had my taste down to a science, and he had been spoiling me left and right with high-priced designer items to wear, handbags, and jewels. I hated a nigga that thought that a white tee and some J's were all there was to life. Grey understood the necessity of fashion and could make damn near anything look good. His broad shoulders, flat stomach, and gorgeous face should have been gracing magazines and televisions all around the world, but the thug in him was strong. And I loved it.

Secondly, he was smart. It was not often that you ran across a true street nigga who used to get straight A's in school and had already finished his bachelor's degree. True, he always had one leg in the streets, but his effort in the classroom was what had eventually led him to becoming the smart business man that he was. He'd earned his B.A. with a major in Business Management right out of high school from Eastern Michigan University, and he continued to seek out and absorb knowledge. Most didn't understand how big of an edge it was to have a college degree behind you, even in the business of selling drugs. It makes it easier for you to hide.

Lastly, well not really lastly because I could go on and on, but Grey had that work. I knew that I was bomb in the bedroom but in the few short months we had been kicking it, Grey had taught me more than a trick or two. Where I normally was dominant, Grey had a way of making me submissive. I catered to his every need and obeyed his every command. There was nothing that he wanted that I wouldn't give to him and vice versa.

I'll admit it. As I watched Grey and my father converse, I knew that I was crazy in love with the thug with the smoky grey eyes. He was unlike any one I had ever encountered. Now that I had landed him officially, there was no way I was going to let him go. Whatever I needed to do to keep him by my side, I would do. Kendrick "Grey" Summers belonged to me.

KIMANI

July 2014

"You're pyscho, bruh!"

I heard the yelling all the way down at the curb where I parked my white 2015 Range Rover Sport. I hopped out and jogged up the driveway to see what was going on. When I approached the door, there was shit everywhere. Clothes, shoes, electronics—all of it broken, bleached, or shredded. Grey was standing in front of the closed front door, yelling and screaming.

"What the fuck?" I mumbled as I picked up a Jordan Flight 97 shoe that was shredded beyond recognition.

"Bruh, today might be the day I go to jail! Over that nutcase in there!"

I saw Grey reach into his waistband, and I rushed over to him and grabbed his arm. He grimaced and tried to yank his arm out of reach, but I held firm. "Aye, you got too much to lose bruh."

Grey looked at me for a few moments as he tried to calm down. His eyes had turned a charcoal shade of gray, a clear indicator that he had crossed the line between anger and rage. His breathing slowed, and he tore away from me. "Look at this shit! All my shit is fucked up because that bitch is mental. She thinks that I'm fucking around with some other chick!"

"Are you?"

"No, man! I got too much shit going on to be worried about chasing down another chick."

"Aight, then. Look, you got more than enough money to buy some new shit, and you too pretty to go to jail. So calm down, nigga. C'mon. Ride out with me."

Grey looked at the mess that was littered across his front porch and lawn and shook his head.

"Yeah, aight. Cuz if I stay here, she's liable to get a hot one in her dome."

We walked to my car and hopped in. I cranked up Future's *Codeine Crazy* and peeled off. Grey rested his head against the white leather headrest and sighed deeply. "I don't know how long I can keep doing this, man."

For the last month or so since he had been fucking with Nakami, all that seemed to emanate from their relationship was drama. If she wasn't taking his phone to try and call unstored numbers back, she was breaking dishes and shit off of some shit she thought she knew about. She never had any facts, but she was always flipping out. I couldn't understand why my brother was putting up with it.

"Why are you?"

"I'm in business with her father. I'm back on."

I skirted past a slow moving car in the far right lane and sped through the yellow light. "Man, what? What about the club?"

"What about the club? You know me, man. The club is cool and so far it's bringing in good money, but it's not fast enough for me. You know I'm used to being that nigga, and I can't be out here waiting to recoup the money that I put into the club. That's going to take too long. Nakami's father is Hero Yukimura, man."

I remained quiet. Blu had told me about Nakami's father, and I had honestly hoped that, after all the shit that went down in Detroit, Grey would have had sense enough not to get knee deep in the game again. But I knew deep down inside that Grey was a hood nigga that couldn't leave the streets alone. As dope as South Beach was, it didn't carry enough excitement to sustain my brother. Plus, stumbling up on a connect so proper was like a sign from God, so I couldn't say that I blamed him.

"Yeah, Blu told me."

"So, what's going on with you two? Ya'll been hanging kind of tough lately." A goofy grin covered Grey's face as he changed the subject.

"I don't know, man. She's cool as fuck. I like her."

Truth was, I was starting to fall for her. But I couldn't tell my brother that. He already thought I was an ol' R&B cupcake ass nigga, and I knew for sure he would clown me if he knew how I felt for Blu after the short amount of time I'd known her. Plus, the way I was feeling about her scared the shit out of me. It was too soon to be so dizzy off a chick, and I had a feeling that I needed to back up for a minute.

"Aw, shit! Look at your ol' cake baking ass!" Grey slapped me on the shoulder and let out a deep laugh. "Nah, for real though. She's a good look. I like her for you."

"Aight, aight. Enough of that shit. We're about to shoot to Westfield Topanga and get you some new new shit, grab some Po' boys from Orleans and York, smash that, and then hit the city tonight. You need to get out." I hopped on the 101-S and headed towards the mall.

"Hell yeah. That sounds like the move. I'm going to hit Jerk and Tyler and see if they're down to roll too."

I nodded in agreement as I drove onto the crowded freeway. Not only did Grey need to ease his frustrations, but I was also in need of a night out. I had been up under Blu since the day we met, and that wasn't even me. She had me gone. There was no way in hell I was going to go out like a sucka. So a night out would do me some good.

✴✴✴✴

"Ol' fashion show ass nigga! C'mon, dawg!" I heard Jerk yelling from downstairs. I could tell he was good and lit, so I knew that tonight would be a wild one.

I passed by the floor to ceiling mirrors that were on the wall next to my bed and double checked my appearance. Dressed in a pair of black, coated slim cut jeans by Diesel, a black, white, and gold Joyrich muscle tee, a black on black Detroit Vs Everybody snapback, and my Jordan Spizike's, I looked damn good. The full sleeve of tattoos on both arms were out. I had been letting my facial hair grow in after the last modeling gig made me cut it, and my boy Jake had my line up crispy. I was normally on my model shit, but tonight I felt like chillin'.

I walked down the stairs and rounded the corner to kick it with my niggas in the kitchen. Jerk, Tyler, and Grey were already taking back shots and had poured me one for every one that I had missed.

"Oh, shit! It's Mani from the block in this bitch!" Grey laughed.

"Damn, nigga! I almost didn't recognize you without ya model make-up on!" Tyler clowned.

"Fuck ya'll!" I laughed.

It felt good to be around my niggas. Jerk was a nigga we had met in college. He was from the Bay and had moved to Michigan to go to Eastern on a scholarship. His real name was Cole Spencer, but he was such an asshole that all the females on campus gave him the nickname and it stuck. Tyler was my brother's best friend from the hood. We all grew up together, and when Grey made the move to L.A., he encouraged Tyler to roll with him. He wasn't a street nigga at all but you couldn't tell when he was hanging with us. This nigga Tyler was as ratchet as they came, but he turned that shit off quick, fast, and in a hurry when it came to work. He was one of the top engineers at Toyota and was definitely about his coins.

I slammed back all five of the Remy V shots that they had poured for me, and we left the house. We decided to take two cars to South Beach, so Grey and I hopped into my Range Rover and Tyler and Jerk got into Tyler's black 2015 Jaquar XK.

We made it to the club twenty minutes later, and there was a line down the block going both ways on the street. The valet greeted the boss and skated past the security, up the elevator, and into the club. My brother had that shit rocking! It was wall to wall people, beautiful bartenders, and bottle girls, and the DJ was going in. It was fine ass girls all over the place in every different shape and color, like a fucking buffet. I was ready to dive in. What I wasn't ready for was the tap that landed on my shoulder.

"Fancy running into you here."

Aw, shit. I knew that voice anywhere. I turned around and came face to face with my ex, Vicious. I just knew tonight was going to get crazy.

BLU

July 2014

I was mad annoyed. I had planned on doing nothing but
propping my feet up and surfing Netflix in my pj's, but Nakami
had stormed up in my condo, breathing fire and raging on about
some fight with Grey. I halfway listened as she ranted on and
on.

"Blu! Earth to Blu! What the fuck?! Are you even
listening?"

"Honestly, I tuned you out after you said you bleached his
clothes. What is wrong with you?" I threw the remote control
onto the couch and walked to my kitchen. I grabbed a bottle of
Arbor Mist Peach Moscato out of the wine cooler and a glass
out of the cabinet.

I was over hearing her talk about Grey. If she wasn't dick
riding and going on and on about how special and perfect he
was, she was losing her damn mind trying to catch him in a lie
or with some other chick. I know that her last relationship didn't
end well, but damn! She needed to ease up.

"Ain't nothing wrong with me! He's the one with the
problem," she pouted as she picked up her phone.

"Kami, you got to chill. Ya'll have been dating for two months, and you already destroying his property? You're going to lose him if you keep this shit up."

Everything I said went out in one ear and out the other. "Oh, so he out partying, huh?"

"What?"

"The gps I put on his phone..."

I cut her off. "You put a tracker on his phone?"

"Yes. And when he left his house, he went to the mall and then back to Kimani's so-"

I cut her off again. "You been stalking this nigga all day?"

She looked at me like I was the one with the issue. "Yes, bitch. Any more questions before we go find this nigga, Detective Buckley?"

"You the one playing the police, hoe!" I snapped. "And what are you talking about *we* going to find him? I'm not going anywhere."

"Yes, you are because I can bet that your man is right by his side entertaining some thot bitch in a Rainbow outfit."

I poured the glass of wine and took a sip to calm my nerves. Nakami sure knew how to get me worked up.

"First of all, Kimani is not my man. We're just kicking it. He can have all the thot pockets he wants. Secondly, you need to have several seats if you think I'm about to run up behind you to chase this man that has given you no reason to think he's doing something scandalous. Find some chill," I said as I rolled my eyes. It was only when I opened them that I realized that I had just been talking to myself. Feeling like my attempts to calm my best friend down weren't registering, I walked to my bedroom where I found her rifling through my walk-in closet.

"The hell?"

"Here. You haven't even taken the tags off this." The dress that she flung my way hit me in the face. I caught it before it hit the floor and put a hand on my hip. "I'm not going."

"Blu. We don't have time to debate this. This nigga probably has some little pop tart twerking all over his lap right now. We need to get dressed and go. Now!" she screamed.

She grabbed a few items from my closet, walked into the bathroom down the hall, and slammed the door. I sighed in frustration because I knew there was no way she was letting up. I really didn't have a choice but to get dressed and participate in this fuckery.

****

Nakami and I hopped out of her Porsche, already faded from hitting the blunt, and she tossed the keys to the valet. It was around 12:45 a.m. when we finally arrived to South Beach and there was still a line around the corner. We bypassed that shit and walked straight into the club as the bouncer recognized

Nakami as Grey's girl. The club was live and, although I had been reluctant to go, I was warming up to the idea of partying the night away. I knew Nakami wanted to hunt down Grey, but I wasn't about to be going on an embarrassing dummy mission with her. So I had called in reinforcements. I spotted them standing by the bar.

"Domani! Yhazmine!" I squealed as I approached my friends.

It had been a while since we had hung out, but I was glad to see that they had made it on such short notice. Domani and Yhazmine were a set of fraternal twins that I had met when I attended community college. Domani stood about 5'5" with dark brown eyes, black shoulder length bone straight hair, and a body like Draya. Her sister, Yhazmine, was around 5'7" with a cute blonde pixie cut, slanted almond shaped eyes, and a body more reminiscent of Ciara. They were both bad as fuck and cool as hell. When they saw me approaching, they screamed and embraced me.

"I'm so glad ya'll made it!"

"Girl, truth is we were already headed here. I heard that this was the new hot spot so we had to check it out," Domani smiled.

"Yeah, you know *my man* did a good job with this place." Nakami walked into our conversation with a satisfied look on her face.

Yhazmine rolled her eyes. "We already know that you're sleeping with the owner, Nakami. No need to flex."

"No flex, boo. I just needed to make sure ya'll understand that he's off limits."

"Anybody that fucks with your crazy ass is just as mental as you are. So you don't even have to worry about that," Domani remarked before she dropped a few bills on the bar. She snatched up her drink and walked away with Yhazmine on her heels.

Domani and Yhazmine did not like Nakami. They put up with her because she was my best friend, but they thought she was a loon and a half. I couldn't blame them. When they first met, Nakami got us kicked out of a restaurant for throwing her food on a waiter who she had suspected spit in it. And that was something light compared to the stuff I had seen her do. Nakami acted on pure emotion 99% of the time and never felt it necessary to get all the facts before she lost her cool. But I had to fuck with her the long way because no matter how out of pocket she got, she always had my back.

I started to walk away to catch up with Domani and Yhazmine, and Nakami pulled on my arm.

"Where are you going?"

"To kick it with them. I told you I would come with you, but I'm not about to be in the middle of your foolery. Handle your business, but I'm going to be over there." I pointed in the direction of my friends.

"Oh, yeah? So you mean to tell me you're not going to check your boo about that half naked slutbucket that's popping her twat in his face?"

I turned in the direction she was staring in, and my heart dropped to the soles of my Giuseppe heels. I had come to the club knowing the situation between Kimani and I was clear on the fact that we were just cool. But as I watched him cozy up to ol' girl, I knew at that moment that I more than liked Kimani. I watched as a very pretty brown-skinned woman, with a weave that touched her ass, wound her body like a snake in front of him. Kimani was on his hood shit, swagged out with a drink in his hand. He looked damn good. I instantly became jealous as he stood and started dancing up on her. The dark haze that had fallen over the club made it hard for me to make her out, but something about her seemed familiar. Before I could stop myself, I was following behind Nakami as she stalked over to their section.

Grey had the booth drowning in bottles of everything from Ace of Spades to Louis XIII. There were women piled into the booth, falling over themselves to compete for the attention of the four fine ass men that surrounded them. Grey was the only one who wasn't dancing on a chick when we walked up. That to me signaled that Nakami had nothing to worry about, but that didn't stop her from going in off rip.

"Really, Grey? You out here trying to catch you a new one?" Nakami put her hand up to mush Grey in the face, but Grey grabbed her wrist.

"What do you see me doing, huh? Pouring a drink is a crime? Kicking it with my niggas is wrong? Yo, you wildin'." Grey roughly let go of Nakami's arm.

Nakami grabbed up the girl that was closest to Grey, pulled her by the arm, and pushed her out of VIP. She went for the next bitch and did the same. "Ya'll hoes gotta go!"

Grey's dark skinned friend, who reminded me of the actor Lance Gross, tried to butt in. "Yo, who is this bitch?"

Nakami threw her hands on her hips. "I'm *his* bitch, nigga! Who are you?"

Grey jumped between the pair, trying to prevent the inevitable from popping off. Kimani finally stopped dry humping long enough to look up and saw Nakami and me standing there. When he saw me, he looked stuck like a deer in headlights. Regaining his composure slightly, he damn near pushed the girl he was with to the floor trying to get to me. I smiled to myself. Unlike Nakami, I was going to play this cool. As Kimani approached me, I side stepped him and went for the girl.

"You good, mama?" I grabbed her arm to steady her balance.

"Yeah, I'm straight. Thank you." She shot a look at Kimani.

"I'm Blu." I extended my hand. She stared at me for a moment before she shook it.

"Vicious." She flashed a smiled.

"Oh shit! You're in that singing group, Wild 1's. Ya'll are dope! That song *Trappin'* is my shit, girl!"

I knew I recognized her face from somewhere. She was his ex-boo or something. I remembered seeing pictures of them together at a few events on my favorite gossip site, Baller Alert. From what I knew, they had a bad break-up so I was a little shocked to see them grinding all up on each other. But this was what you sign up for when you try and date someone who's well known. He was in the industry, and these were the types of chicks that were trying to get his attention. Because of their history, I knew I needed to nip the situation in the bud if I was ever going to stand a chance.

Before she could respond, Kimani interrupted. "Hey, Blu. What... uh...what you doin' here?" He smiled with only one corner of his mouth. Something I noticed he did when he was nervous; cute.

"Oh, you know Nakami," I answered. "Always with the drama. So I had to come and make sure she didn't get into too much trouble."

"I feel that. Uh, hey. Can I talk to you for a second?"

"Oh, I don't want to interrupt..." I looked at Vicious and then back to Kimani. He excused himself and grabbed my arm to pull me away from the booth, leaving Vicious irritated and confused. We walked out of the main area and to the hallway that led to the restrooms.

"Blu, this is not what it looks like. Vicious is..."

I grabbed his chin in my hand and slipped my other hand in his back pocket. I looked into his green eyes for a moment before I ran my tongue across his pretty lips. Not satisfied with just a taste, I leaned in and kissed him deeply. He relaxed against the wall and pulled my body close to his. His strong hands palmed my ass, and he groaned as I moved my hands from his face to his neck and dug my nails into his flesh. Slowly, I pulled away.

"It's cool, baby. I'm not tripping. I'll see you later?"

Kimani licked his lips as he stared at me like he wanted to rip my dress off my body and fuck me senseless right there in the hallway.

"You got that."

"I know I do," I winked at him and walked away in search of Nakami. I knew where Kimani was going to end up after the club let out, so I was no longer worried about him. Tonight I was going to throw this pussy on him so good that he wouldn't be thinking about no damn Vicious. Now I just needed to find my best friend before some shit went down. Lord knows what kind of trouble she had gotten herself into.

GREY

July 2014

I dragged Nakami by her arm to my office in the back of the club. She was struggling to keep up with me in the six-inch heels she was sporting, but I didn't give a fuck. Damn, she was a hot head! On top of coming to *my* house and destroying all *my* stuff, she had the nerve to try to front me in front of my niggas at my place of business? The chick had lost her marbles. I pulled her into my office, and I closed and locked the door.

"The fuck man?! What is your problem?! Haven't you had enough?!" I yelled.

"That's what I should be asking you! You got a chick that's willing to ride with you 'til the wheels fall off and can handle every inch of you in the bedroom, and you still out here bitch shopping?"

I sighed deeply. "Like, all this shit you say that I'm doing...it's all in your head, ma! Like I've told you before, I'm not doing shit. I'm trying to get this money and hold you down. I don't have time for nothing extra!"

On some real shit, I wasn't lying. I hadn't been fucking with anyone else but Nakami since we met. I knew how crazy good my hook-up with her father was, and I wasn't trying to do anything to jeopardize it. She could check my phone and email and even the cameras inside the club. I was all hers, but she had to nip this "girl interrupted" act with the quickness. I liked Nakami, but I loved my money. She wasn't going to mess up my means to an end with her off kilter antics.

I could feel Nakami's eyes on me as I walked around her to sit down on the couch. Damn, she had fucked up a niggas buzz. She stared at me with her hip poked out, and I got the chance to take in her appearance for the first time. Nakami was definitely a bad bitch. With copper colored skin, thick curly hair that was all hers, and a body that could put the baddest of video vixens out of work, she was dope. She was also smart and funny when she wasn't jumping to conclusions, and she could go off in the bedroom. There wasn't anything that was off limits with Nakami, and I dug that.

I stared at her and she stared back at me. As pissed off as I was, I couldn't ignore how horny she was making me. Her stance, her body, that skintight jumpsuit she was wearing…all of it was wearing me down. I felt my anger subsiding, and my little head began to outthink the bigger one. Tired of looking at the black stretch fabric clinging to all her assets, I motioned for her to come over to me. I knew that she was a little off, but my money train had just left the station. I needed to make sure that bitch continued to come. Fucking her in the meantime would be a bonus, as long as she could calm the hell down.

Nakami walked over to me slowly, knowing exactly what I wanted.

She ran her hands down her breasts, as she continued to swagger over to me. I knew she had gotten blowed on the way to the club by looking at her damn near closed eyes. High sex with Nakami was like none other. In one swift move, she popped her big ass titties out of the top of her jumpsuit and began to pinch at her nipples. My dick rose inside my camo pants, so I just leaned back and let him do his thing. At the very least, she owed me some bomb head and a couple hours of straight fucking. I was going to blow her back out until she was out of fluids to release. Put that act right in her system, ya heard me!

GREY

December 2014

I looked down at the stunning six carat, princess cut diamond ring housed in the red velvet box. I shook my head as I realized what I was about to do. Fury began to reign over me as I thought about my current situation.

I'd been putting up with Nakami since the night she made a scene at the club. Yes, *putting up with.* The beauty that had reminded me of Tae Heckard had turned into a nightmare reminiscent of Carrie. She'd gotten too comfortable and turned into the girlfriend from hell. It's like an invisible switch had been flicked on, and it made her go from zero to one-hundred real quick.

She started calling and texting me twenty-plus times a day, popping up at my house, and going through my phone. Her temper is ridiculous, and half the time I have to walk out to keep from putting her ass in a chokehold. She'd sold her downtown loft and moved in with me, uninvited of course, and I'd really gotten to know her. She was bat shit crazy. She freaked out about little shit, and had to have control of everything. She was the definition of a sour patch kid; one moment she was practically salivating at the mention of sucking a dick, and ten minutes later she was trying to bite it off because she thought of something that triggered her to suspect I was fucking with someone else. Like, bro! Everything that I thought I liked about her had disappeared, and this mental patient had taken her place.

And I could see where her crazy came from. Hero was looney toons too. He put me on, no doubt about it. His product was potent, and I had even started carrying more than just coke. Hero had put me on a plug that was able to get me molly, ecstasy, oxy, and this new shit that was a mix of Ritalin and ex that was selling like crazy on the college campuses. I was up to my ears in profit, but Hero had to control every bit of my business. He made me set things up a certain way, deliver things a certain way, and even hire specific people. Any move I made had to be run through him. If someone made the slightest mistake, he was quick to bust his gun or come up with some deranged method of torture for whoever had crossed him. I had nicknamed his ass Jigsaw, the creepy dude from Saw, because he was that fucking nuts. Both of them together had me ready to put a bullet in my own head just to escape.

The cherry on top of the bullshit was that he'd recently started cutting down on the product he was giving me, which in turn slowed down my business. I found out why soon enough. He called me to visit him at his place in Calabasas and asked me why I hadn't put a ring on Nakami's finger yet. Like, bruh!

That bitch was nuttier than a Payday, and he thought that I was going to wife her? That's exactly what he thought. Before I left that meeting, he made sure that he made it clear that my gravy train would be stopped indefinitely until I proposed and got busy making him an heir to his empire. I agreed to his face, but there was no way in hell that I was signing up to put up with that broad 24/7 and pop out some nutty babies with her ass. I had something else up my sleeve that would get rid of all my problems, but it was something that took time and planning. In the meantime, I would have to keep up appearances and actually propose to her. I hated that I had to unleash my dark side, but I couldn't live like this much longer.

Sill angry about having to go through with this bogus ass engagement, I burst out of the jewelry store and ran right into another person. My reflexes were quick, so I was able to grab her before she fell completely on her ass. I helped steady her on her feet.

"My bad. I wasn't even paying attention. You good?"

"Don't even worry about it. I got enough to cushion the fall," she chuckled as she patted her hips.

I looked at her for the first time. Standing around 5'6" with skin the color of melting brown sugar and shoulder length red wine colored hair, she was so stunning that it caught you off guard. I had to close my eyes and open them again to make sure I was looking at a woman and not a mirage. She was thick, and

I'm not talking video vixen thick. She was just thick. Down south, cornbread, and collard greens thick. Probably the type that Drake was always writing about. I couldn't even front on shorty who was dressed in a pair of leather pants, an oversized sweatshirt with the words Money Talks written on the front, tall black leather pumps, and a pair of oversized sunglasses on top of her head. She looked every bit of a stylist as she stood there checking me out on the low.

"I can see that," I smirked.

"Boy, don't be flirting with me like that. I know you gotta crazy girlfriend lurking somewhere in the shadows," she joked, looking around as if someone would pop out of the bushes at any second. I slyly eased the engagement ring box into my jeans pocket.

"Damn, straight like that?"

"Yeah, as good looking as you are, I know you've got some chick whipped and ready to whoop some ass over you. And knowing how big of a flirt I am, I need to get moving before I wind up in some unwanted drama." She smiled, let her shades fall over her eyes, and started to walk away.

I called out behind her. "Can I at least know your name? Gotta pair it with the face I'm sure I won't be able to get out of my head."

She turned around, her hair swinging briskly in the wind, and showed off her pearly whites. Pulling out a business card from her large white purse, she handed it to me. "Maybe when you need a line-up, you can visit me."

She walked off switching, and I watched her disappear around the corner. I finally looked down at her card that read: Blaze McGowan, Celebrity Hair Stylist, Barber, and Luxury Hair Salon Owner. Make your appointment today at Park Ave Salon and Barbershop.

I slipped the card in my pocket, making a mental note to hide it somewhere so that Nakami didn't get her hands on it. I definitely was going to drop in on Blaze. Because Nakami's unstable ass was going to be a distant memory soon.

KIMANI

December 2014

"Babe, you want two strips of bacon or three?" I called from the kitchen.

"You already know my fat ass wants three," she giggled.

I laughed to myself as I lined the baking tray with one more slice of bacon. I popped the pan into the hot oven and closed it. When I looked up, Blu's beautiful ass was making her way down the stairs. Her blue hair was pulled up on top of her head, and her face was clear of makeup. Dressed in an old work out t-shirt and her lace boy shorts, she looked the best I'd ever seen her. She smiled as she walked towards me.

"Aww, look at you being all domesticated. Am I supposed to kiss the chef?" she grinned.

"Oh, you can do more than that." I pulled her into my body by her hand and then picked her up and placed her on the counter. I rubbed my hands up her thick thighs and grabbed hold of her round hips and squeezed. She leaned in and kissed me, as she wrapped her legs around my waist. I could feel myself reacting to her touch and apparently so could Blu.

"Down boy. You can't be burning up my food trying to get to the cookie." She hopped off the counter, and I smacked her on her ass. "I'm going to hop in the shower real quick," she stated as she sashayed out of the kitchen and back up the stairs.

Damn, I loved that girl. Yeah, I said it. And after only six months, so what? A real nigga knows when it's real, and the shit is real deal like Holyfield. She was perfect for a nigga. She was fun and spontaneous, beautiful and business-minded, compassionate and down-to-earth. And let's not even talk about baby girl's body. Shawty had sex appeal without trying and knew how to keep up with me in the bedroom. Whenever I wasn't with her, I wished she was there. Whenever she was with me, I was plotting on how to steal more of her time. She had a nigga wrapped around her finger, and she didn't even know it yet.

I went to grab the eggs out of the refrigerator and heard my phone buzz on the kitchen counter. I reached for it and sighed when I saw the name of the caller come across the screen.

Reluctantly, I answered the phone. "Yo."

"That's all I get when I call you? Yo?"

"What's good? Is that better?"

"What is wrong with you, Kimani? I haven't heard from you in months, and when I attempt to reach out all you got to say is yo?"

I looked back at the stairs, hoping that Blu didn't reappear. "Vicious, what do you want?"

"Oh, now I'm Vicious?"

"Bruh, what the fuck do you want?"

"You know what I want, Mani. I want you."

"That's not happening. I'm with somebody now," I sighed.

"Oh, you got yourself a new bitch?"

"Nah, not a new bitch. A real bitch. So if you don't mind, I'ma to get back to her. Take care of yourself. Oh, and, uh, lose the number."

I hung up the phone glad to have an excuse to dead that conversation. Vicious was one third of the R&B/pop group Wild 1's that I used to mess with. She was wild and crazy and her sex game was dummy, but that was about all that she was good for. If she wasn't working, she was popping pills or partying. That was cool and all, but she had no substance to her. Her life was sex, drugs, parties, and music, and I wasn't about that life.

When she started to see that my interest in her was waning, she tried to hold on for dear life. She started claiming me in public and making the blogs and gossips sites go crazy with ridiculous rumors. I'm not even going to front like the attention that I got from her stunts didn't help put a nigga on the map a little bit. But she was too unpredictable and rowdy for me. I needed my chick to be chill sometimes, and Vicious was turnt all the damn time. I was happy with who I was with and when I finally got around to tell her how I felt, we'd be official.

NAKAMI

December 2014

"Legs moving side to side, smack it in the air. Legs moving side to side, smack it in the air. Smack it, smack it, in the air." I twerked as the sounds of Beyonce's *7/11* filled the air. I felt like Queen B as I moved around the kitchen, gathering ingredients to make my man a five-star dinner. As I reached in the refrigerator, my phone chimed and interrupted my groove. I reached for it and saw that it was Blu letting me know that she was outside.

I dropped the ingredients that I was carrying on the counter and ran to the door to let my bestie in. A few moments later, Blu came sauntering in dressed casually in a pair of high waist Citizen jeans, a grey cropped Alexander Wang sweatshirt that read Wang on the front, and a pair of wheat Timbs. Her now long blue hair was done in a side fishtail braid, and she was wearing the Melody Ehsani hoops I'd bought her for her birthday last year.

"Hey, bitch! What you 'bout to cook?" she asked as she dropped her Celine bag on the kitchen table.

"Nothing for your greedy ass. I'm cooking my *man* filet mignon with sautéed shrimp, garlic mashed potatoes, and oven roasted asparagus. Oh and some cheddar biscuits."

"You better burn, ho!"

We both laughed. Blu took a seat at the bar style island that extended from Grey's kitchen.

"So what's been up, sis?" I asked her. I hadn't really seen or talked to my girl much since our impromptu trip to Grey's club. We'd seen each other here and there and texted, but we hadn't really chilled in a minute.

"A little bit of this, a little bit of that. You know how I do."

"You still kicking it with Kimani?" I asked.

"Yeah, girl," she smiled so wide that I saw her molars.

"Oop! Let me find out! So have ya'll made things official yet?" I pulled a medium sized skillet from underneath the sink and rinsed it out in the sink.

"Oh, no. We're good how we are."

I looked a Blu quizzically as I placed my hands flat on the counter. I didn't get her. She had herself a perfect man, and she was okay with not having a title? Kimani was a cool ass nigga and, from what I could tell, he treated Blu exceptionally well. He was fine, paid, down-to-earth and was in the process of building a brand for himself. I couldn't understand what she was waiting for. She was going to mess around and lose this nigga trying to let him do him.

"You better lock that down. This nigga has over five-hundred thousand followers on Instagram alone. How many of them bitches you think are up in his DM's while you're over here trying to play it cool?"

"Kami, I'm good. We good. We understand who we are to each other, and I don't need a label to define that. We are moving at a pace that I like, and that's good with me."

I laughed to myself. If she likes it, I love it. It couldn't have been me and Grey though. Bitches needed to understand who he belonged to, and I made sure every chick Grey encountered knew he was mine. If Blu wanted to pretend that she was good with keeping it light, I wasn't going to butt in. But I could tell by the way that Blu's face lit up when I mentioned his name that her heart was in deep. She thought she was protecting herself by keeping things simple, but she wasn't doing anything but fooling herself.

"Anyway, what's been going on with you and Grey? I am still in shock that you sold your place and moved in with him. He must be slanging, honey, because you loved that loft."

I scoffed. "Yeah, maybe a little too much."

Blu's eyes widened. I turned away from her and retrieved the chopping board from under the island.

"What do you mean? Please tell me you found proof this time. Spill the tea!"

"I mean…no, not really. I just have this feeling. I've been trying to catch him in something but every time I do, I end up looking stupid. I've been through his phone, his emails, his pockets...and I swear all he does is talk business. I haven't even seen another chick's name in his phone. But I know something is going on. Call it a woman's intuition."

Blu cocked her head to the side. "Girl, I am your friend, and I am going to keep it all the way a hundred with you; you're fucking crazy. Grey is all about you and his money. A blind person can see that. Leave that man alone and just enjoy being his woman. Bitches like you kill me! Always looking for something to be wrong just so you have a reason to show your ass," she giggled.

I quickly got offended. I slammed the large knife into the onion hard, making Blu jump slightly. "Now this is why I don't ask you for relationship advice. When's the last time you were in a relationship anyway?" Silence filled the room. "Exactly. Not never. So don't be so quick to throw advice about a situation you ain't never been in."

"I have common sense," Blu shot back. "So I don't have to have been in the situation to know what's right or wrong or what to tell your deranged ass what you should do. Now if you want to keep your man, you need to rein in the crazy and act like you didn't just check out of an institution."

"You not going to keep calling me crazy in my house, Blu!" I yelled.

I could feel my face flooding with anger. It would be nothing to chuck this knife straight into Blu's flesh, and she was tempting me.

Blu stood to her feet. "Kamikaze, you'd better chill with all that damn yelling. I ain't the one."

I hated that name! She thought I was displaying signs of crazy before, but hearing that name flipped a switch that brought me out of my body and turned me into someone else. Stabbing the wooden chopping board with the tip of the knife, I leaned across the island and got up in Blu's face.

"Bitch, try me if you want to, but you already know how I get down! You feeling froggy, then jump, bitch!" I could see the spit flying from my mouth and landing on her face.

She paid it no mind, as she stepped even closer to me. "I'm going to disregard your outburst because we're sisters, but let it be known that this will be the last time that you talk to me out the side of your neck and I don't bust you in your shit. I'm going to make my exit and save your life, so call me when you're on your meds." Blu snatched up her purse and stalked to the door. After she opened the door, she whipped around to face me. "If you know what's good, you would lock Grey down before he finds out just how coo-coo your ass is for cocoa puffs. You don't want another Shye situation on your hands, now do you?" Blu smirked before she walked out and slammed the door behind her.

"Ughhhh!" I screamed at the top of my lungs as I pushed all the frames, vases, and candles off the foyer table and to the floor.

The mention of Shye's bitch ass only added fuel to the fire that was raging inside me. Shye Bryant was my first everything. Being so up under my father for so long, when I got to college, I didn't know what to do with myself. My first trip to college was actually to an HBCU, Clark Atlanta in Atlanta, GA. I was happy to be away for a while because my dad wasn't there to make sure that I was all about my books, and my attention began to wander from studying to partying.

I met Shye at the school's annual fall pajama jam. He was strolling with his Alpha frat brothers, and I was watching from the sidelines in awe of all the fine, buff young men dancing around with their shirts off. When Shye jumped up and landed a clap between his raised leg and then stomped the floor with force reminiscent of an earthquake, he looked in my direction and I instantly got hot all over. His nutmeg colored skin was dripping with sweat, and I couldn't help but stare at his ripped body that resembled a Greek God. He smiled a megawatt smile at me, revealing his dimples, and an electric shock shot up my spine.

We exchanged numbers that night, and a few weeks later we were official. He was everything to me, and I couldn't have been more in love if cupid had actually shot me with that damn arrow. Everything changed for us during my second semester. Shye became extremely busy with school, his fraternity, and football, while I made my life completely about him. I would skip class to the point where I couldn't even tell you what classes were on my schedule. Instead, I'd spend all day holed up in his room plotting different ways I could please him. At first he was excited that I was at his beck and call, but he quickly got annoyed. His annoyance pissed me off. Once he started distancing himself from me, I started getting suspicious that he was messing with another girl.

I was quick to let any of those hot in the ass girls on campus know that he was mine and that I was more than happy to hand out ass whopping's to any bitch that tried to go against the grain. But only one chick was bold enough to try me. Parker Princeton pranced her baton twirling, rump shaking, band dancing ass right up on my man. To my horror, Shye dropped me like a bad habit. But I wasn't having that. I went out swinging. I won't go into detail about my actions, but just know that it was enough for Shye to call the police, get a restraining order, have me forced off campus and kicked out of school. Not only was I furious but I was embarrassed as hell. I promised that it would be the last time that I got that crazy over a nigga. But lo and behold, I could feel myself going there with Grey.

Even though I didn't want to admit it, Blu was right. I needed to reel it in and stop acting like a damn nutcase if I wanted to keep Grey around. Since I didn't have any proof that he was messing around, I buried the thought of him cheating in the back of mind and put a lockdown on the crazy juice I had currently been sipping. I loved Grey more than I had ever loved a man, and I needed to make sure that he would be a permanent fixture in my life.

GREY

December 2014

I twirled the velvet box around in my hand for the umpteeth time. I had never felt sicker to my stomach than I felt now. Standing in the bathroom of the Hotel Bel-Air, I could feel myself about to lose my cool. There was nothing I wanted more than to walk out of this hotel and leave Nakami and her fruit cake ass father far behind. But I couldn't. The money that I was making with Hero was far more than I had been making in the D, and I had a far wider reach. I was perpetrating a boss nigga before; now I *was* one. I couldn't give that up. I'd be damned if I ran away from good money because my ninty-nineth problem actually was a bitch.

And a pyscho bitch she was. I almost didn't make it here to the dinner that was taking place outside these doors. A nigga was damn near behind bars off Nakami. I placed my hands on the white marble countertops as I thought back to the events that took place earlier today.

"Grey?" The shrill of her voice let me know that I had some explaining to do.

Huffing, I got up from the living room couch, adjusted the volume on the sound system, and calmly walked towards the kitchen where I knew Nakami was. When I walked into the spacious kitchen, I eyeballed the fuck out of Nakami. Her back was turned, and all I could see was her perfectly round ass hanging out of a pair of grey sweat shorts. The thought of running my hands underneath them was abruptly cut short when she swung around with a deranged look on her face.

"What?" I asked. Just the look on her face alone irritated me.

"What is this, Grey?" She held up a bottle of wine and wiggled it in the air.

"A dildo. What the fuck does it look like?"

"Oh, you got jokes? Well, since you think it's comedy hour in this bitch, I got a riddle for your ass. Let's see if you think this shit is funny. What's flat and broke and scratched all over?"

I waved Nakami off and started walking back towards the living room. I didn't have time for her bullshit today. I was already going to have to put up with Hero in a public setting, so I didn't have the patience for extra shit.

Beep. Beep.

The sound of my car being unlocked caused me to stop in my tracks. "What's flat and broke and scratched all over?" The riddle played through my head a few more times before I bolted out the door and opened the garage. My brand new, onyx black, 2014 Aston Martin Vanquish was now sporting four flat tires, a busted windshield, and numerous scratches to the body.

"Are you fucking..." I walked closer to the car to survey the extensive damage that had been done. I had brought this baby home only three days ago, and it was completely damaged. Behind me I could hear Nakami laughing her ass off. Before she could get another giggle out her mouth, I was in her face with my hands around her throat and her body pinned up against the open door. She barely put up a struggle. In fact, I swear she smiled the entire time. Reality hit me like a brick when I heard a dog bark close by. I released her from the chokehold and pushed her inside the house. I didn't need my neighbors all up in my business.

"Why?!" I shouted.

Nakami stood calmly in the foyer mirror, surveying her neck for bruises. "Oh, now it ain't funny is it?"

I remained silent and clenched my fist together. In my mind, woman beaters are pussyies, but Nakami was encouraging the beast in me to come out and play. And that nigga didn't care if you were a man, woman, child, dog, cat, or God. You could get it just like anybody else could.

"Who you been entertaining in my house, Grey?"

"My house," I corrected her.

"Minor details," she said with a roll of the eye and a shrug. "Who have you been entertaining in my house?!"

"Nobody."

"Nobody, huh? Then whose wine is that in the refrigerator?" She put her hands on her hips.

I looked at her just as crazy as she was. "What?"

"The wine, Grey. You drink red wine. Gaja Barbaresco to be exact. I don't drink wine. I prefer champagne. So what little rat bitch have you had up in OUR crib whose taste level is only at an Arbor Mist level?"

I looked at Nakami for a moment before I walked off. I was liable to knock her head clear off her shoulders at this point.

"Oh, so you just going to walk away while I'm asking you a question?"

"You really off your shit, you know that?" She just stared at me. "When ya homegirl Blu came over here a few weeks ago, what did she bring with her?" Nakami didn't respond, so I continued, "Let me go ahead and answer that for you; she brought over a bottle of blackberry merlot by Arbor Mist. Kept trying to get you to try it because it tasted like juice." I walked up on her. "You remember that?"

Nakami didn't say anything, but the look on her face let me know that she did remember. I wasn't letting up so easily. "DO YOU REMEMBER, OR NAH?!" I screamed. Nakami jumped at the bass in my voice and tried to shrink away like a little kid. "Naw, bring that ass back here." I grabbed her arm and yanked her back towards me.

"Ow, Grey! You're hurting me."

"I don't give a fuck. You just damaged a damn near $300,000 car…no, damn near $400,000, since I had custom work put in on it. And you crying because I'm sinking my nails into your skin? Fuck outta here, man."

She wiggled a little, trying to get out of my grasp, but I held firm.

"I don't care where you get the money from. Whether you take it from your own personal stash or you go crawling to your daddy, you will be replacing that car out there. No, you can't get it fixed. Scrap that shit. Buy me a brand new one just like it. All custom everything. Since you think this shit is a game."

Nakami bit down on her lip, and her eyes filled with water. I was annoyed by the audacity of her to try and shed tears off of a situation her crazy ass has put herself in. Finally, I let go of her arm and walked off.

"Baby, I'm sorry! I just thought that…" She begged and pleaded with me to forgive her for the next few minutes, and I tuned her out. I had come this close to choking the life out of her and ruining everything that I had built in the last few months. I didn't know what needed to happen, but I needed to get a leash on this broad before my whole plan went up in smoke before I had a chance to put it in action.

That ordeal had happened less than eight hours ago. Now I had to swallow my pride and get on one knee. My patience was running thin, and I was damn near ready to bust my gun and jeopardize my money flow to get rid of this migraine named Nakami. But I ain't no quitter. For nothing. So I was going to take a deep breath and go back out there to that dinner and secure my future.

KIMANI

January 2015

"Steph, man, look. I need to be on that show. Whatever you need to do to put me on or get an audition, do it. That's what I'm paying you for. Please don't call again unless you have good news, ma."

I hung up the phone and tossed it on the couch in frustration. Conversations with my agent had been more stressful lately. Seems like the TV industry only wanted to hire models as background niggas, and I ain't never been a background nigga. The fact that I had been working my ass off at these acting classes and working privately with an acting coach added more angst to my frustration, because I felt like I had the juice and nobody was willing to give me a chance.

Knock knock.

Who the hell? I was not in the mood for company. Begrudgingly, I pulled myself off the couch and answered the door. Blu barged in, attacking my lips with force. I almost tumbled over as she barreled her way in. I pulled back from the kiss, holding on to both of her arms and looked at her strangely.

"What the hell, Blu?"

She huffed. "What? I missed you."

I threw her the side eye and let go of her. Closing the front door, I walked past her and back into my large living room, heading straight to the adjacent bar.

"Who pissed in your Cheerios?" she asked.

"Why are you here?"

"What do you mean? I just told you I missed you." I heard her fall into the plush leather sofa behind me. I reached for the bottle of Remy V and poured myself a double shot without asking Blu if she wanted one.

"Blu, I ain't spoke to you in two weeks because when I asked you to be my girl, you dipped in the middle of night and started ignoring my calls. You wanted to be done. That's what I got by your actions. So we're done."

"Can you get out your feelings? It wasn't nothing personal, Kimani. It was just-"

"Nothing personal?" I laughed and then threw back my shot. "It was all personal. I ain't been in a relationship in damn near five years, I choose you as the person that I want to be with and you get ghost? You can stay ghost, bruh."

I was irritated now. Blu was a cold piece of work in every sense. She was bad than a mothafucka. Body tight, skin a beautiful muted shade of caramel, sexy brown eyes, and lips like pillows. She was also a damn acrobat in the bedroom, a gourmet chef in the kitchen and she made her own money. But her heart was locked in a cold ass ice box that she refused to let me melt. Blu had waltzed into my life, opened me up, and shut me down in a matter of six months.

She'd done everything I'd wanted my woman to do except commit. And I don't know why she wouldn't! I knew she wasn't seeing anyone else. But I'm not chasing behind a chick. I don't have the need to. I got chicks on speed dial that can take care of every need I may come across, so the fact that Blu was playing a nigga was laughable.

We'd been seeing each other since Grey's club opening and, unbeknownst to her, I had fallen for her on the spot. Not to sound like a fruity ass nigga, but something in me felt the need to show her love. To give her all of me. And I felt like I had. Apparently, she either wasn't ready for someone to love her or she ain't recognize a real nigga when he presented himself to her. Either way, I'd done all I could to show her and I wasn't about to continue to look dumb.

"I never said that we were done!" Blu popped up from the couch.

"Your actions said enough." I walked back to the bar, prepared to pour myself another shot. I felt her presence and the smell of her Marc Jacobs perfume simultaneously. She ran her long decorated fingernails up my chest and pressed her face against my back. I hated that I felt some type of way about this girl. My dick jumped in my sweats, clearly more excited about her presence than my heart was.

"Baby…" she whined.

I wiggled out of her grasp and poured another shot. I hated that her voice sent goosebumps through me and I kept envisioning her pouty lips all over my body. But fuck her, bro!

"Don't act like that, Mani. I was just…surprised. And confused. I didn't see it coming."

"You didn't see it…" I stopped talking because I felt the anger mounting. "Aight. You've had time to think about it. So are you going to be my woman?" I felt like a sucker for even asking again.

She opened her mouth to speak, but nothing came out. She stood there staring at me searching for the right words but there were none. She didn't want the commitment, and I was tired of just fucking her. I'd been there and done that with my fair share, but I was ready for something more stable. But I knew I shouldn't have to force her. I was twenty-six, paid as fuck, handsome as fuck, dope as fuck, building myself a legit brand… and this confused bitch didn't know a catch when she saw one? Okay, I didn't mean to call her a bitch. But she was right; I was in my feelings.

"Don't even worry about it, ma. That's the last time I'm going to ask. If you need to get your stuff from here, feel free. But I got shit to do soon, so you'll have to make it quick."

I took the second shot and downed it, slamming the glass against the bar before walking away. Blu grabbed my arm roughly, and I looked at her like she had lost her mind. "Blu, don't embarrass yourself, ma. You wanted to make your exit, so that's what I'm allowing you to do."

"That's not what I wanted. I just want to continue how we are." She looked like she was on the verge of tears. My first instinct was to change my mind about letting her step. I wanted to grab her ass and fuck some sense into her, but I knew that she was too closed off for me to change how she felt right now.

"And I want you to be mine. What are two stubborn people to do?" I shrugged my shoulders. "Not to be rude but-"

She cut me off. "You got shit to do. I hear you, boo. Loud and clear."

Without another word, she turned around and walked away. I couldn't stand to watch her go, so I headed upstairs to get dressed, wishing that she had decided differently.

GREY

March 2015

Sweat dripped off my forehead and plopped right onto the curve of Nakami's back as I stroked her. Her ass was tooted to the perfect angle, and I was trying my hardest to control my nut and let her get hers first.

"Oooh, G. Yesss," she groaned.

Swinging her head around to look at me, she began to throw her ass back on me, matching the rhythm of my thrust. She clenched her muscles around me and rolled her hips, making me squeal like a little bitch. I bit down on my lip and closed my eyes, careful not to look at her face because I knew for sure that I would bust on sight. I felt a dread fall loose from my ponytail, and I hastily threw it off my face. I thought I had finally willed my nut away for a few more seconds until Nakami knocked my hands off her ass, bent forward so that her head was damn near in-between her knees, and used her hands to spread her ass wide.

"Fuuuuckkk," I hissed.

See, the thing about crazy bitches is that their sex game was fire. Good girls always wonder why we can't seem to leave the crazy ones alone, and this was that exact reason why. Keeping her position, Nakami started to buck wildly and the sound of her ass slapping against my body caused me to grip her hips, dig my nails into her flesh, and release all up in her. I knew I didn't want her nutty ass having none of my kids, but my small head overruled my big head at the moment and I couldn't help but marinate inside her for a few more minutes. We finally collapsed onto the bed, and she wiggled her way over to me and laid her head on my chest. I rolled my eyes. I wanted nothing more than to push that bitch off me and dip, but I had to keep it together.

"You want something to eat, babe?" she asked sweetly.

"Naw, I'm good. I just want to chill for a minute."

Nakami got up and walked out of the room stark naked. I could feel myself getting hard at the sight of her and tried to talk myself out of it. The more dick you provided, the crazier they get. And Nakami was already missing a few screws, so I wanted to stop sexing her. But I knew if I did she would get suspicious, and I didn't need those types of problems either.

My phone buzzed, shaking me out of my thoughts, and I reached for it. Surprised, I sat straight up in the bed and answered the call. "What up, bro?"

"I can't call it. What you on?" Kimani's voice rang through the phone. This nigga had been MIA for a couple weeks, so I was little shocked to hear from him.

"On chill."

"Fa sho. Aye, you want to hit this little event with me real quick? It's an industry thing and I got a plus one and shit."

"What? You ain't asking Blu to accompany you?"

"Man, I don't even want to get into that. We done, bro."

"Damn, what happened?"

Nakami walked back into the room with a bowl of strawberries, a glass of ice, and a bottle of champagne tucked under her arm.

"She just ain't trying to be tied down. I was putting in work, trying to get her on my team and she played me off like my name ain't hot or something. I'm not feeling that, bro."

"You should be- AHHH!" I jumped at the unexpected sensation on my manhood. "What was that?"

I looked down and Nakami was buried in-between my legs with a cube of ice between her teeth. She rubbed the ice up one side, flicked the ice cube into her cheek, and deep throated me, creating a cold to hot sensation that almost made me drop my phone. Damn, she was cold with it! The only good thing that had come out of proposing was the new bag of sex tricks she had unleashed on a nigga. It was like once she had that rock on her finger, she became a porn star. My knees buckled, as she used her hand to stroke me in rhythm with her mouth.

"Bro, you there?" I heard Kimani ask.

I opened up my mouth to respond, but I felt the tip of her tongue at the base of my dick and the only thing that could come out my mouth was a hiss.

Kimani laughed. "Aye, you need me to call you back?"

"Na…Nah. I'll be there, bro. Just shoot me the info."

"Bet."

I disconnected the call and tossed the phone on the bed ready to concentrate on the work that Nakami was putting in. But as soon as I hung up, Nakami stood and wiped her mouth.

"Where you bout to go?" Attitude was dripping from her tone.

"Are you serious right now?"

"I'm deadass. I put a hot meal on the table and just finished fucking and sucking you senseless, and you think that you're about to hop your ass on to the next bitch? You got me all wrong!"

"First off, you can miss me with the dramatics. Second, my brother wants me to ride with him to a networking event. So it's not even like that."

Rolling my eyes, I walked away from her and to the bathroom to get in the shower. Although I hadn't really been in the mood to go out, I was relieved that my brother had called because I was liable to kill this broad with my bare hands if she kept this shit up tonight. I was over her ass! And to think I just raw dogged her! I needed to get my shit together.

I heard footsteps approach the bathroom and tried to rush to lock the door. Nakami was too quick and pushed open the door, damn near hitting me with it.

"Bitch, is you crazy?!"

I hadn't meant to call her out her name, but it was what I had been referring to her as in my head for months now. Guess it just slipped out.

"Nah, but *you are* if you think that you're going somewhere tonight!"

I ignored her as I turned on the shower and tested the water with my hand. Feeling like it was the right temperature, I stepped in and closed the door. Nakami stood on the other side butt ass naked, her body shaking like a raging pit bull.

"So you just gonna ignore me?"

I remained quiet as I lathered myself with soap and zoned out to a tune in my head. After a few moments of silence, I turned around to find that Nakami had disappeared. *Finally,* I thought. I finished showering in peace and hopped out to dry myself off and lotion myself down. Creeping into the bedroom, I found it empty and that made me nervous.

Quickly, I threw on a pair of leather 7 For All Mankind jeans, a clean white v-neck, and my Citizens brand distressed denim jacket, and slipped into my black Cole Haan boots. Next I hurriedly sprayed myself down with some Dior cologne, grabbed my silver three-karat studs for my ears and my phone off the bed, and walked out of the bedroom in search of Nakami. To my surprise, she was nowhere to be found. Not in the kitchen, living room, game room, patio, or theater. Shrugging my shoulders, I snatched up the keys to my newest baby, a rose gold painted 2015 Audi R8, and headed towards the garage. When I got to the garage, I realized that Nakami's car was missing. Crazy hoe must have found something to distract herself. *Whatever*. I thought to myself. I hopped in the car, plugged the address into my GPS, and got ghost.

****

I pulled up to the W Hollywood about a half hour later with Drake's *Energy* putting me in the right state of mind for the evening. I let the valet handle my car and took the elevator up to the rooftop pool where the event was taking place. Cali had made it easy for me to fall in love with my move because the weather was exceptional damn near all year round. In the middle of February, it was a crisp sixty-one degrees at 8 pm, and that was much more than I could say for the D right now.

I reached the rooftop and was guided in by a pretty young chick with her cheeks spilling out of her white booty shorts. She showed me to a cabana where my brother was seated, surrounded by a couple of baddies. He hopped up when I approached the booth.

"Bro, you made it!" He seemed a little on, as he greeted me with dap and a hug.

"Nigga, barely," I replied as I shook my head.

"Why? Nakami's ass was fooling again? I don't see why you don't just leave that broad alone."

"Probably the same reason you don't wanna leave Blu's ass alone."

I followed him over to the bar area that was already packed with people.

"Nah, homie. For one, Blu and I are done. Two, our situations are completely different. I wasn't messing with Blu because I needed something from her. I was trying to get her on my team because I actually loved her. You holding on to that crazy bitch because you need her."

"Ah, so I was correct in assuming there was a crazy female waiting in the wings?" a voice slithered into my ear. I turned around and came face-to-face with the beauty from the other day.

"Such a pretty woman really doesn't need to be a stalker," I joked.

"Boy, please. You're fine and all but I don't need to chase," she smiled.

I was captivated by her confidence. Dressed in a butterscotch colored jersey dress that skimmed her curvy body and stopped at her knees, and a pair of brown lace up sandals showcasing her pretty pedicured feet, she looked drop dead gorgeous. Her hair was wavy this time, seductively covering half of her face, and her make-up was light and subtle. If I was one of those niggas that believed in all that romantic shit, I would've thought that I'd already fallen in love without knowing the first thing about ol' girl.

"Blaze, right?"

Before she could respond, Kimani jumped in. "Excuse my rude ass brother, I'm Kimani." He extended his hand for her to shake. She obliged.

"Nice to meet you, Kimani. I'm Blaze. I see that good looks definitely run in the family. You're gorgeous." I took notice of the dimple in her left cheek as she grinned.

"Thanks, ma. You're quite stunning yourself. Are you a model?" he asked.

She laughed and flicked away a loose strand of hair. The tiniest movements that this woman made had me on brick.

"Modeling what, honey? While I appreciate every inch of my body, the modeling world doesn't."

"Well, you could model for me any day of the week." I eyeballed her body like it was USDA prime steak.

"Both of you are too much. What brings you all to my event?" she asked.

"Your event?" Kimani balked. "What do you do, Miss Lady?"

Blaze held up her finger, asking Kimani to hold on, and spoke to a few people that passed by her. Kimani looked at me with a raised eyebrow, and I knew what he was thinking. But I'd be damned if this nigga tried to get on first. From the moment I laid eyes on her that day I bumped into her outside the jewelry store, she was mine. I hadn't made a move on her yet, but I was still trying to get rid of Nakami and her father before I started anything with someone else. But Blaze had never left my mind.

My brother rubbed his hand and mouthed, "Game On," but this time I wasn't trying to compete. Kimani and I always played this game of who could get on first, but Blaze wasn't a game to me. I had plans to make her mine as soon as Nakami was out of the way. There was something about Blaze that intrigued me and made me want to be with her, and this was only the second time we had spoken. Some might say that I move too fast, but I just know what I want when I see it. Why waste time?

Blaze turned her attention back to us. "Sorry about that. To answer your question, Kimani, I'm a business owner, celebrity hair stylist, and barber. I throw this annual event for entertainment professionals to have a fun place to network and make connections."

"That's dope." I was in awe of her.

"I'm glad you think so. But I must admit I had ulterior motives for stepping to you all tonight."

"If it involves being able to be in your company for the rest of the night, I'm wit it." Kimani licked his lips.

"Well, actually every year we do some kind of fun activity during the event to raise money for a charity. This year, we're doing an auction."

"Oh, you need a donation? I got you." I reached into my jeans and pulled out the wad in my pocket.

"No, it's actually more than that," she giggled. "It's a date auction. We put some of our entertainment professionals up on stage, rattle off a list of their attributes, and let our wealthy attendees bid on a date with them. I just lost two of my male auctionees, and you all are guaranteed to bring in some big bucks. So what do you say?"

"For you baby, you got it." I smirked at Kimani's smooth ass after he made that remark. He was delusional if he thought that he really had a chance. Blaze was feeling a nigga, and Kimani's too pretty ass wasn't going to cure her need for a thug in her life. I could tell that she needed a nigga to handle her pretty, thick ass, and I knew for sure that she thought I was the man for the job. But I wasn't going to burst my bro's bubble just yet.

"Perfect. You can follow me and I'll have my assistant ask you a few questions and tell you what you need to do." She started walking in the direction of the stage and we followed her, watching her ass sway the entire time.

NAKAMI

March 2015

Grey had managed to piss me all the way off! The audacity of this mothafucka to think that he could just ignore me! I had something for his ass though. Fuck getting off the crazy train, because apparently niggas just don't know how to act. Currently I was parked in front of the W Hotel where the GPS tracker on Grey's phone alerted me he was. Crazy thing was I had an event that I had planned that was taking place in the same hotel, so I was curious to see what this nigga was up to. Now that he had proposed, there was no way in hell I was letting another bitch come claim my spot. All I know is if I find out this nigga had got a room to sex down one of his jump offs, I had my .32 in my purse ready to set some shit off.

The GPS only told me that the phone was located in the W, but not where inside, so I was going to have to do a little sleuthing. Dressed simply in a pair of Saint Laurent biker jeans, a v-neck boyfriend tee, a nude colored blazer, and matching So Kate red bottoms, I made my way through the lobby and towards the front desk. Before I could get there, I heard my name called.

"Nakami! You made it!" I whipped around and saw my client, Blaze McGowan. She skidded over to me in some bomb lace-up gladiator sandals and wrapped me in a hug.

"Hey, B. How do you like how everything turned out?"

"It's perfect. I never worry when you're in charge. You're the shit at what you do, and I always have complete faith in your vision."

"I'm glad that you trust my skills that much."

She grabbed my arm and pulled me over to the concierge. I started to protest but she started speaking before I could get anything out.

"Excuse me. I have the event on the rooftop and was wondering if I could get some matches or a lighter or something. Some of the flames on our lanterns have gone out."

The concierge nodded and walked away. I liked Blaze. I'd been working with her on different events, big and small, for about three years. She was a dependable client who was always at meetings on time, paid on time, and didn't give me a headache with constant changes or differences of opinion. She gave me an idea and let me run with it, only giving her input when necessary; and that was the best kind of client. Blaze was also just a cool chick in general, and I never minded hooking her up when she needed something last minute.

"I know you probably just came to check on the event, but you should stay for the auction! I have some fine ass men that are going to be coming to the stage and, even if you aren't in the market to buy, you can damn sure window shop!" she laughed.

Before I could respond to her, I felt my phone buzz. It was Blu. I contemplated whether or not to answer. We hadn't spoken since the day that we argued, and I still had no desire to speak to her, especially not while I was on a mission. I sent her ass to voicemail.

"Sounds interesting." I raised my eyebrow and eased my phone into my back pocket.

"It is, girl. I have my eye on one of them, so I'm going to get my check book, honey. The auction starts in twenty minutes, so please grab a drink and come sit at my booth." The concierge came back with a few books of matches and handed them to Blaze.

"Ok. I'll do that."

Blaze strutted away, and I walked over to the main desk with a lot on my mind. I felt like Grey was slipping through my fingers. He was my soul mate; I could feel it in my bones that he was the man for me, but I felt like things were slowly starting to change. I was doing everything right. I was keeping him fed, fucked, and fly, and I still felt like that wasn't enough for him. The fact that I bust it wide open and this nigga decided he'd rather be running the streets than hitting back shots on the baddest bitch in the city blew my mind. I just didn't understand.

And Blu had the nerve to tell me that it was because I was crazy. First of all, this nigga hadn't seen crazy yet! I had been popping my Xanax like Altoids since we'd started dating in order to control my mood. So if niggas thought I was one flew over the cuckoo's nest now, let me run out of my meds.

After attempting to find out if Grey had made reservations at the hotel and coming up empty handed, I decided to go check out the party. I needed to make sure that my work was impeccable even in my absence. When I arrived at the rooftop, I was pleased to see that, although Tristan was the human version of a migraine, she actually had a natural gift for event planning and had managed to pull the event together the way that I wanted.

The rooftop pool area of the W was a sea of coastal colors like sand, ocean blue, muted coral and off white and strings of colored glass lights hung above the open air space creating a starry night. There were printed ottomans scattered around and tall wood lanterns serving as extra mood lighting. There was a catered buffet along the wall serving gourmet Hawaiian barbeque and seafood and two full bars on either side of the venue. There was a small stage towards the front of the venue that my client was using for an auction. Her turn out was nice, as it had been the last two years I had planned it. After checking in with Tristan and doing a walk-through, I walked up to the bar. I didn't know how to find Grey, but I'd be damned if I had followed him all the way here and didn't find him.

"What can I get you to drink?" The handsome bartender flashed me a wide smile.

"Crown Royal on the rocks with a splash of apple juice."

As the bartender went to tend to my order, the announcement of the beginning of the auction caused me to turn around. Blaze was on the stage with a mic in her hand, dressed in a completely different outfit. For as curvaceous as she was, her style and fit of her clothes were immaculate. Dressed in a pair of silver sequined joggers, a black lace bustier that cinched her waist, and a pair of bad ass Casadei studded sandals, homegirl looked bomb. I'm not a hater; I give credit when it is due, and Blaze was definitely a bad chick.

"Here you go, miss."

I turned around briefly to grab my drink and slip the bartender a tip. Turning my attention back to the stage, I watched as Blaze excitedly introduced the first auction.

"Now, ladies, I have to let you in on a little secret. There was another fine gentleman who was going to gift you all with his presence, but I bid on him behind closed doors and let's just say my $5,000 donation will be more than just a tax write-off," Blaze laughed.

I walked over to her booth, which lent itself a clear view of the stage.

"Ok, so let's start with the men…my favorite, as you can tell," Blaze giggled. "Ladies, get out your check book or your credit card, because this man is definitely going to make you want to spend it all. Coming to the stage is one of the sexiest models I've ever seen, Kimani Summers!"

My eyes nearly popped out of my socket when I saw Kimani stroll onto the stage. *What the fuck?*

He winked at Blaze and went to greet the growing group of women that had settled at the base of the stage.

"Kimani is a world renowned male model who has graced the pages of numerous magazine and billboards. He's currently branching out into the acting world. Kimani is twenty-six, with no kids, no girlfriend, and he has a banging ass body!"

Kimani lifted his shirt up and stuck his tongue out, revealing his chiseled chest and abs. The women went wild. I rolled my eyes as women started calling out numbers before Blaze could get her next sentence out. I was not only pissed that this nigga was out here playing my homegirl like this, but I knew that Grey's ass was around here somewhere. He'd better not have been sniffing up and behind none of these ratchet hoes or thinking that he was going to get his ass up on that stage to get sold to the thirstiest bidder. Fuck that.

I slammed my glass down on the table adjacent to the booth and was about walk out to find Grey when I bumped right into him. He looked too damn good to be around all these thirsty bitches and my attitude flared immediately.

"Grey, what the fu—"

He placed a kiss on my lips and silenced me. I looked at him quizzically, and he returned the look. "What you doing here, babe?" he asked.

"Fuck you mean, Grey?"

He laughed, "I mean when I left the house, you were gone and all of a sudden you pop up where I'm at? I never told you where I was going."

"I'm here because this is my job. I planned the damn event. Why would you be here? You running behind your thot of a brother, huh?" I shoved him in his shoulder.

Grey grabbed my hand and pulled me away from the group of people inside the booth that were beginning to stare.

"I'm going to tell you this one time and one time only. That ratchet shit; you twisting your neck and flinging your finger in my face like you really about to do some shit, you better dead it. I don't put my hands on females, but you really need to stop acting like you don't know who the fuck I am in these streets. "

His words came out like a sheet of ice, and his eyes glazed over looking like cold, shiny steel. I could see the muscles in his jaw flexing, so I knew he was beyond mad. But for what? He had some damn nerve.

I snatched away from his grasp. "What the fuck ever, Grey. I'm going home. And I suggest that you don't be too far behind me, unless you forgot who you're fucking with. One wrong move, and you're done in this game. I can guarantee it. So play with me if you want to, nigga."

Angrily, I marched away from him and out of the door that led back to the hotel. I was steaming. How dare he try and front on me like my father don't hold his life and livelihood in his hands? I didn't want to threaten him like that, but I had had about enough of him trying to play me for stupid. He better wise the fuck up, or he really was going to be assed out.

BLU

March 2015

I wanted to take a shot of Remy so bad. Fuck a shot; I needed to throw back the whole damn bottle. Instead, I sat on my couch draped in blankets, holding a tub of Haggen-Dazs Rum Raisin ice cream, watching it turn into flavored milk. I couldn't even bring myself to eat it; that's how in my feelings I was. Tears had been leaking from my eyes for hours. I was surprised that there was anything left, but they kept falling; dripping down my face, and soaking the blanket on my lap.

Two Months; that's how far along I was. The one thing I swore I never would be was a baby momma, and here I was about to bring a baby into the world by myself. And the fucked up part is that I had a feeling that if I hadn't walked out on Kimani that night, he would have been overjoyed at my news. I'm so stupid! What was my problem? As I sat their wallowing, my brain forced me to think back to New Year's Eve night.

"You're giving me that look," I giggled. I took a sip of my champagne and looked over the glass at him. He moved from the kitchen to the bar to fix himself a drink while the TV showed Nicki Minaj tearing down the stage at Dick Clark's New Year's Rockin' Eve special in New York. Grey and Nakami had invited us to the lavish party Grey was throwing at South Beach, but

we had decided to avoid the madness and the drama that followed them and just kick it at Kimani's place. I was content with that. I watched him make his drink and silently drooled over his shirtless back, memorizing the muscles and tattoos.

"What look, girl?" he took a sip of what I was sure was D'usse and set his glass back on the bar.

"That look that means that you want to fuck me right here and right now."

Kimani walked over from the bar and pulled me off the couch. I sat my wine glass on the coffee table and wrapped my arms around his neck. We swayed back and forth like there was a smooth R&B classic on, even though Nicki was rapping her heart out to a hip hop beat.

"Don't be trying to act like you know me," he whispered in my ear before he took a quick nibble. I squealed and tried to pull away, but Kimani held firm. I twisted around so that my back was to him, and his arms were holding me tightly around my waist.

"I don't want to fuck you, though."

I smiled, turning my head to the side so that I could see his face a little. "Oh, no?"

"Naw, I want to make love to you." The words rolled off his tongue so smooth that I laughed.

"Oh what? You love me now?" I laughed. I just knew that the buzz from the wine had hit me.

"I do."

Now that shit stopped that giggle before it could get all the way out. I whipped around to face Kimani. He stared back at me with a straight face. I tried to pull away again, and he held me closer.

"Stop trying to run away from me ...from this. You do this every time I try to tell you how I feel. What are you scared of?"

"Kimani, you can't love me. We haven't known each other that long and I-"

"What does that have to do with anything? If I'm standing here telling you that I love you, then I do. You know me well enough to know that I don't say things I don't mean."

My whole body started to shake. This couldn't be happening. I wasn't ready! I opened my mouth to speak, but Kimani's lips covered mine before I could utter a word. Passion transferred from his body to mine, sparking flames that I never knew existed. This unexplainable feeling swept over me, leaving me breathless and caused me to break the kiss. Kimani didn't seem to mind as he zeroed in on my neck and ears. Once I began to feel hot all over, he pulled back. My eyes shot open.

"Your head might be holding you back from loving me, but your body and your heart is already there," he breathed.

I started to dispute his claim. But before I could, he swept me off my feet, wrapped my legs around his waist, and carried me up the stairs. He planted soft kisses all over my face and neck until we reached his bedroom. He let me down, and I started to take my shirt off until he stopped me.

"Let me do all the work."

Slowly easing his hands underneath my cotton tank top, he lightly grazed my nipples with his thumbs. That simple action caused shivers to bolt up my spine and for me to let out an involuntary moan. He continued pushing his way up and removed my shirt by pulling it over my head. Kneeling, Kimani unbuckled my jeans and eased them over my hips, down my thighs, and past my legs, kissing each place as he passed it. In one swift move, Kimani yanked my boyshorts off, ripping them from the seams and eliciting a shriek from me.

"Lie down," he commanded.

I obeyed him and lay across his California king sized bed, feeling nervous about sex for the first time ever. I don't even remember feeling like this before I got my cherry popped. But for reasons unknown to me, this man had my emotions doing all kinds of crazy things. The sound of Tank's Can I filled the room, and the recess lights dimmed. I felt Kimani's presence near me, but I didn't see him.

"Sit up real quick."

I sat up and turned to his voice. He kneeled onto the bed and slipped a satin eye mask over my head.

"Kimani, what the hell? I'm not into that 50 Shades of Grey shit."

"Just trust me."

As soon as the words escaped his lips, I felt my body being yanked towards the edge of the bed. My legs went up in the air and were then pushed out to the side. It was killing me that I couldn't see him and that I couldn't determine what was coming next. I lay there listening to Tank serenade me as the anticipation of what was to come lingered. Then I felt him.

His lips covered my second set, and he tongued me down like my core was a well in the middle of a desert. His tongue explored every dip and curve, every crease and crevice. He was expertly skilled in oral acrobatics. I knew this from previous sex sessions, but this time felt different. It felt like he was trying to send me a message through the movement of his tongue without using words. He grabbed ahold of my hips and pulled me closer to his mouth, and he feasted. He licked and sucked on my clit like it was the last meal he would ever have. I writhed and bucked against his tongue like I was riding a mechanical bull, and he never lost rhythm.

Ecstasy was something that I thought was made up. Just an imaginary word used to describe the unexplainable or the mythical. Gottdamn if this man ain't prove me right. There weren't any other words accurate enough to describe the feeling that was coursing through my body. I rolled my head back involuntarily, taking in all the pleasure that Kimani gave me. Without warning, he stopped, and a few seconds later I felt him enter me.

Even behind the veil of darkness, I saw stars. His strong hands gripped my waist and pulled me towards his body, allowing him to drive deeper inside me. I couldn't hold back the moans that tumbled out my mouth, as he slowly piped me down. I was used to that back breaking-hair-pulling-sweat dripping-sore bodied fuck, but Kimani was now giving me a new experience. He was taking care of my needs and paying attention to every sensory point that existed in my body, leaving no part of me untouched. With every stroke, he explained his feelings for me. I didn't have to look at his face or hear his voice to know what he was trying to say. I felt it all.

The tears started falling down in sheets as I reminisced. I remembered every sight, sound, smell, and taste from that night. I wished I could go back and change the way things ended. That night after we made love, I lay in the bed trembling. I was so scared. Emotions were hitting me from the left and the right and I was just…scared, man. So when I was sure that Kimani was in a deep sleep, I tip-toed out his house and fled the scene. He'd done the unthinkable and the impossible, and it fucked me up. And here I was two months later, looking at a sonogram of our love child, and I had no clue what to do. When I found out about the pregnancy, I tried to reach out to Nakami. But being the stubborn bitch she is, she sent me to voicemail. I had tried to visit Kimani, to feel him out, but he wasn't feeling me. He wanted something that I didn't know if I could give him. As much as I wanted to let him know that he was going to be a father, I wasn't ready for a second dose of rejection. Everything was so messed up, and I didn't know how to fix it.

The next morning I woke up in the same spot on the couch, still holding onto the carton of warm, melted ice cream. I forced myself off the couch, dumped the carton in the trash, and walked into the bathroom. I looked a hot mess. My hair was all over my head, the bags under my eyes could have held a month's worth of groceries, and my lips were chapped and peeling. I didn't feel like doing anything about it either. But I realized that I only had one move left, and I had to act on it fast. So I hopped in the shower and got myself together.

It was almost noon by the time I exited my condo. Dressed in pair of drop crotch sweatpants, a black, cropped Civil crewneck sweatshirt, and a pair of liquid metal Nike Dunk Sky Hi's, I felt refreshed and optimistic about my next option. I hopped in my Land Rover and drove over to South Beach, hoping that I would be able to catch Grey at work.

GREY

March 2015

I rolled my eyes as I watched the screen of my iPhone 6 light up. This was the third message that I'd received from Nakami in the last twenty seconds. I hit the ignore button and went back to looking over the numbers from last night. By no means did I think that my club would be anything less than popping, but it had far exceeded my expectations. In the last couple months, South Beach had hosted three fashion shows, forty celeb birthdays, twelve after parties, and six album release parties. South Beach had become the hot spot in LA, and I was bringing in so much money that I had to come in on my days off to sort through it.

Hustling for Hero, although stressful as fuck, was also lucrative. The amount of drugs I had floating around Cali, as well as Arizona and Nevada, had my pockets overflowing. We'd taken over the universities and the block, and we'd even busted up in the corporate world. But I was still having the same damn problems with Hero and his crazy ass daughter. I was at my wit's end. The plan was already in motion, but it was a slow burn and I was starting to lose patience. I wanted them gone! The fact that Nakami had the nerve to fucking threaten me like some hard-headed child made me want to lay hands on her on her last night for real. She had no clue how close she had come to being a victim on the First 48. She was just lucky that the drive home was able to calm me down and that she was knocked out when I got home. Because if she hadn't been, I would've been more than happy to rock her ass to sleep. My annoyance with her started to resurface when I heard my phone going off for the fourth time.

"If this bitch don't fall back…," I mumbled.

A light knock at the door attempted to further annoy me. If this was Nakami, I swear before God…

"Hey, boss. I know you said no interruptions, but she said it was urgent." My club manager, Trickie, poked his head through the door. I started to protest until he opened the door wider and revealed that was Blu and not Nakami. Surprised, I stood up to greet her.

"You good, bro. She can come in."

Trickie nodded and stepped back, letting Blu through. She smiled shyly and waited for Trickie to close the door.

"What's up, Blu? Whatchu doing here?"

Blu and I were cool, but I wasn't sure why she had just popped up at my club. She was a dope little chick and much more level headed than Nakami, but her and Kimani hadn't been fucking with each other for a few months. It's not like I was bothered by her presence; I was just curious.

"Hey, Grey," she said as she nervously wrung her hands.

Now I had never known Blu to be nervous. During the many times that I've been around her, I had witnessed her be bold, brash, unapologetic, and forward. So this timid and shy Blu had me thrown for a loop.

"You want a drink or something?" I asked her.

"No, no. Uh, do you mind if we step outside, though? I...I..." she started fanning herself and turning a little pale. I didn't know what was going on with her, but she looked like she might pass out any second. So I rushed around my desk and walked her out to the patio of the club. Blu inhaled deeply several times before she turned to me with a weak smile.

"You good, ma?" I asked, genuinely concerned after that little episode.

"Well... I'm pregnant."

NAKAMI

March 2015

My breakfast came flying out of my mouth in liquid form as soon as I got to my car. Never had I been so hurt that it actually made me physically sick. But I guess hearing your best friend tell your fiancé that she was pregnant would do that to you. Fucking bitch! How could she do that to me? She knew how I felt about Grey, and she just couldn't help but shake her big ass all up in my man's face. I knew she was a gutter ass hoe, but I befriended her anyway. In the past few years, I'd starting having a gnawing feeling that she wasn't feeling my booming business, my luxury condo, and my fresh-off-the-showroom-floor whip, but I honestly thought that putting her on and having her manage the strip club would squash all that. Apparently her jealousy was more deep rooted than I could imagine.

I tried to push thoughts of her fucking my man into the back of my head, but then I remembered; the warning about Grey, her not wanting to commit to Kimani…the fucking Arbor Mist. THE FUCKING ARBOR MIST! This bitch had been coming for my man the whole time! But it wasn't just my man that she wanted. She wanted my life, and she was willing to do the grimiest shit she could think of in order to plop her fat ass in my spot. She one upped me. She was going to have my man's baby before I could even attempt to get pregnant. My best friend was having my fiancé's baby.

Having that thought pass through my brain caused me to gag. This time I was able to catch myself before the rest of the contents of my stomach came spewing out, and I quickly hopped my ass in my car. This was unacceptable. I could feel the wrath brewing inside of me as I turned the key in the ignition and skirted off. I didn't know what the fuck I was going to do about the situation. But whatever I decided on, these primary color named mothafuckas were going to regret fucking over a chick like me.

GREY

March 2015

"You are? That's great, sis!" I grabbed Blu up in a hug and spun her around. Thoughts of her about to pass out a few minutes ago entered my mind and I quickly put her down.

"My bad, yo. But damn! I'm going to be an uncle. That's dope!" I was genuinely excited for her and my brother. But the look on her face told me that she still hadn't come to terms with the situation.

"It *is* my brother's baby, right?" I asked with a little more anger in my voice than I had intended.

"Of course it is!" she shouted. "I just... I don't know..." she stuttered.

"You don't know what, ma?"

"Kimani and I aren't really speaking right now, and I don't know if he'll be as excited about this baby as you are."

"I understand you're nervous about telling him. But if that's his kid, he has a right to know, Blu. Fuck all that lovey dovey shit ya'll been mad at each other about. Regardless of whether or not you want to be in a relationship with him, Kimani needs to know." I grabbed Blu up around her shoulders and brought her close to my body.

"I know my brother. And I know he's hurt because he really loves you. But he's going to take care of his kid, no matter what ya'll are going through."

Kimani and I were raised by a single mother who held down jobs like a Jamaican to make ends meet. Our low-life daddy only came around to hit and quit my mother on a semi-regular basis. When that nigga was done busting one, he walked out the door without even acknowledging our presence. He never claimed us, touched us, hugged us, or provided for us. As kids, we couldn't understand why. So I knew that Kimani would never leave his own seed out there without a father if he was alive and able to be there. That just wasn't a part of his make-up.

"I hear you, Grey. I do. But I don't know how to do this. I love him. More than anything or anyone I've ever loved in my life. But I just can't give him what he wants." Blu sniffed as tears dropped like rain drops from her eyes. "I'm going to tell him, but I can't face him yet."

"Whatchu mean?"

"I'm going to go away for a little bit, just a few weeks at most.   I need to get my head together, wrap my mind around the idea of having a kid, and think about how I want to approach this for the sake of our child."

I let go of Blu and looked at her, confused.

"Go away? Man, what the hell is that going to do? Ya'll women, I swear."

"It may not make sense to you, but it's all that makes sense to me. Please? I promise I won't leave Kimani hanging for long. I just need some time."

I stayed silent for a moment. I never kept anything from my brother, even though we weren't as close as we once were. But looking at how distraught Blu was, I was willing to allow her some time to pull it together...especially if it meant that my brother would get another shot at the girl he was in love with. I'm a thug with a heart...what can I say?

"Yeah, man. I won't say shit. But you've got two weeks. Kimani is already going to lose his head when he finds out you dipped, but you can't have me lying to my brother. Get your thoughts together and bring your ass back here," I warned.

Blu nodded her head, and I could only hope that she was taking me seriously. I had eyes and ears everywhere that I needed them. If she violated, I would not hesitate to drag her ass back to the city.

NAKAMI

March 2015

I currently had a plan. It was shaky at best, but it would have to do because it was all that I had. In the end, I still wanted Grey to be my husband. Fuck the bullshit, my hoe ass friend and that bastard baby. I had never loved someone as completely as I did Grey, and I wasn't going to let that go just because my so-called bestie didn't know how to keep her vagina to herself. She would pay dearly for her fuck-up. But first, Grey would need to learn a lesson.

I pulled the rented Nissan Altima into Kimani's driveway and parked. I was relieved to see that he was home. Quickly, I exited the car, dropped a few eye drops in my eyes, and shook my head. I approached his front door and knocked. I took a few deep breaths and shook the jitters out of my system. He opened the door with a shocked look scribbled across his face.

"Nakami, what are you doing here?"

"I… I…I don't know what to do!" The waterworks were in full effect, as I grabbed him and cried on his shoulder.

I could feel his body tense up against mine, and I smiled to myself. This was going to be fun.

"What's wrong? What happened, ma?"

"He… I…," I fake stuttered.

"Hey, hey. It's ok." Kimani pulled me into his house and closed the door behind me. "C'mon." He led me into the living room of his beautiful home. The black Italian leather sofas, rich mahogany wood fireplace, and cherry wood floors made the living room look masculine and expensive. You could tell that he'd hired an interior decorator by the style of the plush grey rug on the floor, the patterned throw pillows, and the odds and ends that littered his coffee table and bookcases.

I sat down on the couch and attempted to wipe the tears away. He noticed and hopped up.

"I'll get you some tissue. Hold up." He jogged out of the room and returned a few seconds later with some Kleenex. "You want something to drink?" he asked.

I sniffled for effect, glad that he offered. "Yeah, I'll have whatever you're having."

He walked off to the open kitchen and roamed the refrigerator. "All I have is milk, bottled water, and wine. Unless you want something stronger than that."

"After the day I've had, I'll take something dark on the rocks. You might want to make yourself one too. You're going to need it," I said, hoping that he didn't decline.

A few moments later, he returned with two glasses of what smelled like Hennessy. I took one from him as he sat down next to me. I observed him move, and I could understand the appeal. He was prettier than I normally like my men, but there was no mistaking his good looks. The tattoos that traveled from both his arms to the base of his neck added a much needed edge, and his sparkling green eyes looked like exotic oceans that any woman would gladly take a dive in. Although I was purely here on a mission, I smiled inwardly at the pleasure I was going to reap from the pain that had been caused.

"So what's going on, ma? Talk to me?" Kimani looked at me over the rim of his glass.

"I don't even know how to put this into words." I started the tears back up.

"C'mon, stop crying. Just tell me what's going on."

"Blu's pregnant," I blurted.

Kimani's already pale face turned damn near clear once those words came out my mouth. Unsure of what to do with himself, he lowered the glass to the coffee table, then raised it back towards his lips, then finally placed it on the coffee table. Abruptly, he stood up and walked away from the couch with a confused looked painted on his face.

"I know you're her girl, but what does that have to do with you?"

"It's Grey's baby."

The look on Kimani's face almost made me want to cry real tears. His face dropped down to the Maison Margiela shoes on his feet, just as I imagined his heart did.

"What did you just say?" he muttered.

"Please, don't make me say it again," I clutched my stomach, as if it pained me to speak on it.

Kimani bolted out of the room and up the large iron staircase.

"Kimani!" I shouted.

I got no answer, so I took that time to initiate phase two. I reached into the pocket of my light trench coat and pulled out the bottle of prescription sleeping pills. Inside, I had an already crushed pill that I dumped into Kimani's drink. I used my finger to stir the contents and quickly took my seat on the couch after hearing Kimani come back down the stairs.

He was frustrated. "She's not answering the phone," he huffed.

"Did you think that she would? Grey told me ya'll weren't talking before you found out, so why would she answer now?" I countered.

"Does she know that you know?"

"No."

Kimani paced in a small circle. "Man, what the fuck?" Suddenly I could see the fire in his eyes and, before I could stop him, Kimani grabbed his car keys off the coffee table and headed towards the door.

I hopped up and ran behind him. "Where are you going?"

"To find Blu!"

"She's gone!" I screamed. Kimani stopped in his tracks but kept his back to me. "I went by her house before I came here. I sat in the car for a half hour trying to talk myself out of killing her, and she came out with two suitcases and hopped in her car."

Kimani remained silent for a moment, then he shrugged his shoulders. "Fuck it, then. I'm going to go find my brother's bitch ass."

He opened up the door, and I reached for his arm. I cued the crocodile tears and got ready to hit him with everything I had. I'd never been into theatre, but I had always been with the dramatics. "Please! I know you're upset, but so am I. I don't have anyone else to turn to. I can't tell my dad because he would murk that nigga on site, and the one person I would normally turn to is the cause of the bullshit." I could feel Kimani's muscles relax a bit as I held on to his arm. "Please."

Slowly, Kimani closed the door and turned to face me. He studied my face for a moment and then sighed deeply. "I gotchu, sis."

I smiled weakly and walked back into the living room with Kimani following behind me. He tossed his keys back onto the coffee table and picked up his drink before he sat back down on the couch. I kicked my shoes off and curled my feet underneath me. Kimani looked into his glass, and my heart rate picked up.

I couldn't see any remnants of the sleeping pill from where I was sitting and was hoping that he couldn't either.

"I can't stand warm liquor. I'ma go grab me some more ice. You want some more?" he asked.

"No, I'm good. Thanks."

Kimani walked out of the living room and back into the kitchen. I breathed a sigh of relief as I heard the ice machine spit out a few cubes. Kimani returned a few moments later with the same glass of Hennessy. He surprised me when he threw the entire contents back in one swallow before plopping down heavily onto the sofa. A weary look wavered in his eyes, as he glanced at me and then trained his gaze on the empty glass.

"How'd you find out?" he asked.

I watched as he leaned back onto the sofa with his eyes closed. The pills I had were potent, and I knew that they would kick in almost immediately. As I began to talk, I could see him begin to fade so I loosened the belt on my trench. It was time for phase three.

GREY

March 2015

I was like a kid approaching the candy store. I had been so caught up at the club with the books, then Blu, then organizing the pick-ups from the trap, that I almost forgot that I had my date with Blaze tonight. Yeah, I had a date with another chick and I didn't feel the least bit bad about it. Nakami had been past worn out her welcome, fake fiancé or not. I was closer than ever to deading that situation, and I was happy to have Blaze to take her place. I had to be careful, though. I didn't need another Nakami on my hands.

I walked past the mirror that adorned the hotel suite I was paying for and made sure that I was fresh. Dressed in a pair of Paper Supply jeans, a button down denim shirt by the same designer, and a pair of beige suede Christian Louboutin Amory boots, I was definitely clean. I finished off my look with a pair of beige suspenders that were casually hanging off my hips and a grey scully that housed my dreads that were in need of a re-twist. I had sprayed myself with Clive Christian cologne on the way out the bathroom and threw on my favorite watch, the Dover by Jord. A nigga was looking and feeling good, like a boss nigga should. I had told Nakami that I had to shoot a quick move out of town for business and, surprisingly, she didn't put up a fight.

Happy than a mothafucka, I walked out of my room at the Mr. C Hotel in Beverly Hills and took the elevator to the restaurant downstairs. Instead of being seated and waiting for Blaze inside the restaurant, I chose to wait for her in the lobby of the hotel. I stood around for less than ten minutes before she sauntered in the door. The dictionary didn't currently have a word fit to describe this woman. Fuck the restaurant, I was ready to make her my full course meal on site. Blaze sashayed over to me in a black leather skirt that started at her waist and stopped at her knees with a sheer black lace top that showed off the top of her stomach. Her perky breasts that were spilling out of her bra. A white leather jacket was draped over her shoulders, and her hair was pulled back from her face in a low ponytail. Simple but large diamond studs hung from her ears, and multiple rings sparkled from her fingers. Unconsciously, I reached up and wiped the corners of my mouth, sure that I was drooling at this point.

"Hi," she smiled coyly.

I didn't respond with words. I reached down and wrapped her up in a hug, making sure my hands made their way to the top of her backside. She smelled like cinnamon and peaches and it made me brick up instantly. I pulled back hoping that she couldn't feel my dick being childish.

"You look good," I complimented her.

"So do you."

I stared at her for a moment and watched as her cheeks flushed. All of a sudden dinner at a Beverly Hills restaurant sounded offensive. She deserved better than a five course meal at a four-star hotel.

"Yo, I got an idea. I'll be right back. Stay right here." I smiled and dashed off before she could protest.

A few minutes and a couple phone calls later, I returned to where Blaze stood, confused. I smiled mischievously, grabbed her hand, and led her towards the door.

"Where are we going? I thought we were eating."

"We are. Just not here."

Outside the hotel, there was a car waiting for us. I motioned for the driver to stay in the car, while I opened the door for Blaze. She hopped in, and I followed suit. The driver took off, as he already knew where we were headed.

"So, Blaze, tell me about yourself."

Instead of answering, she rebutted, "So, you're really not going to tell me where we're going?"

"Do you trust me?"

She stared at me with a look of amusement on her face. When she realized I wasn't joking, she cleared her throat and looked me square in the eyes. "Against my better judgement, I do."

I laughed a little. "Why against your better judgement?"

"C'mon. My first run in with you, you were coming out of the jewelry store carrying a ring box in your hand, *though you tried to hide it.*" I coward under embarrassment as she continued, "And when I ran into you the second time, your brother hinted to the fact that you were using a chick for a come-up. Don't play me like I'm stupid, cuz I'm not," she frowned.

Damn. She had just read me my rights. I didn't even know shawty had peeped the ring box. I had to set her straight for that last comment real quick though. "Yeah, you got me on the ring but that situation is in the process of being corrected."

"Corrected? Why does it need to be corrected?"

I sighed. "Because shawty was a bad move. I thought I had come up real quick, but I really had set myself up for disaster. There were some perks that came along with being with her, but that's not why I went after her in the first place. She…she's just a bad move. Let's leave it at that."

Blaze nodded her head. I could tell that she had more questions, but I was grateful that she was able to leave it at that. I grabbed her hand, and she looked up at me.

"Don't think that I'm not sincere because of my situation. Honestly, if I could just walk away, I would. But it's not that simple. I have to make moves quietly before I can be done with it. But I like you. I'm intrigued by you. So if you're with it, let's enjoy each other's company and see what happens from there."

"That's cool on one condition."

"And what's that?"

"Don't lie to me. I need you to keep it real with me. I know that you have a situation, and I can't lie and say that I'm completely okay with it. But I'm willing to see where this goes."

A wide smile snaked across my face. She didn't know how happy she had just made a nigga when she said that. I grabbed her hand, and she pulled it back quickly.

"I'm serious, Grey. Trust that I do fine by myself and I haven't had any problem finding a man that comes without all the baggage that you currently find yourself lugging around. You need to make a choice soon about your lil' situation, or I'll make a choice to dip."

"I believe you. I'm handling it. Just give me two weeks, and you're all mine."

Blaze smiled and then she caught herself. "You don't know me from the thot down the street. Why are you willing to ditch your fiancé to take a chance on me?" she questioned.

Before I answered her, I took a second to think about it myself. Knowing the hell I had gotten myself in by rushing into things with Nakami, I couldn't help but think I was dumb as fuck to be putting myself in the position to make the same mistake twice. But I couldn't help but feel like this move may be my best move. There was something so real about Blaze. She was right; I didn't know her well and we may need to take things slow. But I wasn't willing to give her up.

"To be honest, ol' girl was on her way out before I even met you. And I'm not planning to propose again anytime soon, but I'd definitely like to get to know you more. You're beautiful and confident, you got a mouth on you that turns me on, and you take care of business. I'm attracted to you off rip, and I have a feeling there is more to you than meets the eye."

Blaze grinned and then rolled her eyes slightly. "You have no idea. But like I said before, I trust you. But I'm holding you to what you said. I'll give you a week, but that it."

"You got that, ma."

The car finally pulled to a stop. The driver got out and opened the door for Blaze, while I hopped out the other side of the car to join her.

When I reached her side of the car, excitement was painted all over her face. She looked from the private jet that was parked a few feet away and then back at me with wide eyes. "What is this? I thought we were going to dinner."

"We are. You told me you like Mexican food, right?

"Yes..."

"Well, what has had better Mexican food than-"

"Mexico?! We are seriously going to fly to Mexico for chips and salsa?" she laughed.

"And maybe some huevos ranchero too. We'll come back in the morning, if that's cool."

"You are just too much." She couldn't contain her grin. Blaze grabbed my hand and pulled me towards the plane. "We're going to Mexico, baby!" she squealed.

I couldn't help but feel like that nigga. I knew Blaze could do for herself. But feeling like I could do something for her that no other nigga could do made me feel good. At that moment, I knew that I needed to make good on my promise. The timeline on getting rid of Nakami had just been moved up.

NAKAMI

March 2015

"Whaaa....diddddddd....youuuuu...." Kimani slurred.

"Shhh."

Slowly, I let my trench slide off my body and to the floor. My birthday suit was on full display as I stood in front of Kimani. Quickly, I made my way to the belt on his jeans, on a mission to get this over with. He made a feeble attempt to stop me, but I swatted his hand away and continued to get him out of his pants.

Once he was completely bottomless, I pulled his dick out and began to stroke it. I was happy to see that he was just as blessed as Grey. He began to harden in my hand, and I took that as my cue to hop on. I straddled Kimani and lowered myself onto his thick pole.

"Na...na....what are you doing? You can't..." Kimani tried to lift me off of him, but he was too weak. The sleeping pill had put him in a relaxed state, and he was in no condition to put up a fight.

"I'm sorry I had to drag you into this, bro. But Grey needs to learn a lesson. You can't go around fucking your bitch's best friend and think that you'll walk away unscathed. Ohhh..." I started to feel his dick hitting spots that sent small chills down my spine.

Kimani's hands fell limply by his side. I picked them up, placed them on my ass, and held them there. I knew in my head that I was only fucking his brother for one purpose, but the curve of his dick was fucking up my train of thought. I bounced up and down on his rod like it was my day job a few more times. I could feel myself getting dick dizzy and I slowed my pace as I tried to regain my focus.

Leaning over, I grabbed my phone from the other side of the couch. Turning on the video feature, I propped the phone up against one of the throw pillows and hit record.

As I continued to fuck my fiancé's brother, my mind began to wander. Grey needed to know that I was not the one to fuck with. He might have just thought that I was just some spoiled little princess who only knew how to plan events, but there was much more to me than that.

My father, being the single parent that he was, took me everywhere and involved me in everything. I had mastered jiu-jitsu by the time I was twelve, conquered goju-ryu karate by fourteen, and had also been taught the art of fencing and archery. By eighteen, I was a perfect shot and could throw knives like a motherfucking ninja. While I didn't know how to cook drugs, I did know everything about the back end of the business. I was aware of every crook and crevice of my father's business and, whether Grey knew about it or not, I knew his operation like the back of my hand. I could fuck his entire world up without having to even involve my father.

The only thing was, I was truly in love with Grey; madly, deeply, completely in love with Grey. He was perfect. He was rugged and handsome with good dick and deep pockets. He was a thug with refined edges, incredible taste in clothes, and good conversation. He was smooth with it, smart as shit, and a low-key romantic. He was everything. He only had one flaw in my eyes. He had wandering dick syndrome.

Why couldn't he just keep it in his pants? He had more than enough pussy at home! He could get it anyway that he wanted, any time of the day, anywhere that he requested. I would drop everything I was doing in order to please this nigga, and that still wasn't enough? I sucked him dry, fucked him into a coma, wiped him down with a warm towel, and even stayed up to cook his ass a meal after he got his nut off. I couldn't figure out what in the hell I wasn't giving him that he found in Blu's stank ass!

Speaking of that bitch, she had it coming too. After all the shit that I done for her, she had the nerve to bounce her ass into my bed and onto my man's dick. Did they sleep together once? Or had this been an ongoing thing? Had she fallen in love with him? Was she even planning to keep the baby? These were all the questions that I wanted to know the answer to, and I planned on getting the answers sooner rather than later. The shit I had said about Blu dipping was only half true. The bitch had attempted to skate without me knowing, but I had got to her and put a gps tracker on her car. Blu hated planes, so I knew wherever she was trying to escape to, she was going to drive there. Once I caught up to that hoe, I was going to let her have it; baby or no baby, she was going to feel my wrath.

My grind sped up as I felt an orgasm peaking. I didn't know if it was because of the dick I was currently receiving or if it was because I felt some type of way about the revenge I was planning to get. There was no way that the people that had crossed me wouldn't pay for their sins. I had been taught better than that. My father always said that if you don't show a person repercussions of their mistakes, they are bound to make the same mistake twice. Once I was done with them, they were going to wish that they hadn't made the first mistake at all.

BLU

March 2015

The tears fell again against my wishes. I tried to talk myself out of crying, but apparently that didn't help when you're pregnant and emotional. I had been driving aimlessly for the past six hours, and I had no idea where I was going. I hadn't even really been paying attention to the street signs and highways I was seeing and taking. All I knew was that I had to get out of LA for a minute. I need to think about things, and I didn't need any distractions or anybody forcing their opinion down my throat.

What was I going to do? That was the main question burning inside me. I'd grown up without a family, tossed in and out of foster homes until I aged out at eighteen. I didn't know the first thing about taking care of anyone except myself. I was selfish and self-absorbed, and I couldn't fathom taking care of another human being. If I had this baby, I would be responsible for its life, its choices, and how they viewed the world. I would have to give advice, feign off the boogeyman, and remember to be the tooth fairy, the Easter bunny, and Santa Claus. That was a big responsibility. One that I'd never experienced. I didn't know how it felt to have someone to love and genuinely care for me. Except for Kimani.

That was the other thing. His love scared the shit out of me. How could a person who had never had love in her life accept love from a stranger? To me that was asking to get hurt. Kimani thought he knew me. He loved Blu: the business woman, the quick-witted smart ass, the thick redbone with crazy sex game. But would he love me if he knew who I really was? Would he fall in love with the abandoned kid that nobody wanted? The former stripper that tricked to pay her bills? The reformed klepto who used to steal any and everything just for appearance's sake? The shiesty bitch that used to set up her tricks and snatch valuables and money and disappear? He didn't know me. He knew who I let him see. And I doubted that if he knew who I truly was at heart he would want shit to do with me.

I also had to think about his career. He was a public figure who was gaining notoriety in the entertainment business. Kimani was trying to crossover to acting and was already having issues breaking in the business. I didn't want to add a gun-toting, ex stripper/thief baby momma to the list of reasons why he couldn't get on. I didn't want to become his headache.

A car swerved in front of me causing me to hit my brakes, and it pulled me out of my thoughts. Instinctively, my hand flew to my stomach and that quick threat of danger made the tears flow even harder.

I couldn't deny that the idea of having a baby was growing on me, regardless of the many reasons mounting against me having it. I was so confused. I definitely needed time to sort this all out. As I looked up, I noticed the highway sign. Looks like I was headed to Arizona.

GREY

March 2015

"C'mon, get in!" Blaze smiled as she ran off into the clear blue ocean. I drooled over her body that was covered in an all-white risqué swimsuit. She was gorgeous, fun, spunky and amazing. We'd went to a dope authentic Mexican restaurant and ate until we burst, and then went bar hopping in Cabo. We danced on the beach, took shots, and fell asleep in each other's arms in the white sand. This morning we woke up and hit some shops and then headed to the beach. I had initially chartered the jet for a one night stay, but seeing Blaze enjoy herself had me wanting to stay a few more days. I wasn't ready to leave her or Mexico yet.

Just as I was about to put my phone down and join her in the water, it buzzed. I looked down at it and answered immediately. "Yo."

"We picked up the deposits. Store three was short on product and guap."

"Call the accountant. Have him look into the last three months. Then call the janitor. We need a clean sweep. When I get back, I'll have the store redecorated," I spoke in code.

He was telling me that one of our traps had come up short. I gave him the order to have the whole trap grabbed up and taken to my warehouse, so that I could find out who the culprit was. I didn't have time for the games. Since the timeline on my plan had been moved up, I was going to be taking over shortly and I didn't want any fuck-ups or thieves in my camp. If someone was stealing from me knowing that Hero's crazy ass was on my head, they gave no fucks. They had to go.

"You got that."

"Aye, do me a favor. Keep this between us for now. I don't need him tripping."

"We clear, boss."

I hung up the phone and set it down. I needed to get back to the states to tend to business soon. But for now, I was going to extend our vacation and chill. This mini break from Nakami and her father was so necessary, and I wanted to enjoy every moment of peace before all hell broke loose.

NAKAMI

March 2015

"Arizona, huh?" I smirked.

I was at home on my computer watching Blu's movements. Phase one, two, and three were complete, and now phase four needed to be put into action. I had left Kimani at his crib, dick out and everything, and sent him a copy of our sex tape. I wanted him to know that we had gotten revenge on his brother and Blu. I felt that Kimani was too soft to really do anything. So in order to hit Grey and Blu where it hurt, I needed to drug him and make the video. I knew he wouldn't go along with my plan, but it was necessary. He may even be mad about it, but this plan was going to prevent his brother from being murked by my father. It was either I take care of it or my father takes care of it. And while I knew Kimani was upset about what his brother did, neither of us really wanted his brother to die behind it.

Phase four may be more difficult for him to swallow, but it needed to happen. The gps system I had installed had proven to be super beneficial, but I had to make my move now before anyone else found out where Blu had gone. I knew it was just a matter of time before one of the brothers found out where she was hiding out at, and I needed to get to her before they did. I pulled my Chanel carry-on bag out of my closet and tossed in a few essentials. I could buy whatever else I needed when I got there. Quickly, I searched Priceline for a quick flight to Arizona and looked for their best hotel. I made my reservations and was out the door in thirty minutes.

****

"Hey, babe," Grey answered like he didn't have a care in the world. *Bastard.*

"Hey. I just called to let you know that I need to handle something for my father for about a week. So I'll be out of town."

"Oh, word. Ok, cool. Hit me when you touch down."

"I will. Love you."

"Yup, you too."

He hung up the phone, and instantly my heart started to break. He hadn't even asked me where I was going! He was distracted and it was probably that fucking baby on his mind! Oh, this bitch had to go!

I had just landed in Phoenix, Arizona and had rented a car. I drove to the Canyon Suites at the Phoenician and checked into my room. I had a few things I needed to do before I could get at Blu, so I quickly changed into the only outfit that I had brought with me; a pair of ripped Joe's jeans, a simple white t-shirt, a pair of grey Chuck's and a grey, white and black flannel I tied around my waist. Grabbing my white Sally LaPointe leather bomber, I walked out of my room in search of the items I needed to get down to business.

Three Days Later

GREY

March 2015

My impromptu vacation with Blaze was over. To keep it real, a nigga was kind of sad. I wasn't sure how I was going to continue to see Blaze in the city with Nakami's nosy ass on my head, and that only made me want to handle her even quicker. She was still out of town, but as soon as she touched down in LA, she was done. Spending the last couple days with Blaze had solidified my decision to get rid of Nakami. It was a shame because, even though she was crazy as fuck, she didn't really deserve to die because of it.

Her emotions got the better of her, and that caused her to act on impulse and assume shit that wasn't actually happening. She was fucked up in the head—trust— but I had been halfway in love with her looney ass at some point and that made me feel some type of way about killing her.. But Hero *had* to go, and she rode hard for her father. Once I got him out the way, there was no way that I could keep up a relationship with Nakami, even if I wanted to. She would find out who was behind his death if it was the last thing she did, and I didn't need her gunning for me. So I was getting rid of all of my problems once and for all.

"Grey, my son." Hero reached out for a hug. I rolled my eyes as I embraced him and then sat down across the table.

Every Tuesday we met at the same restaurant, sat at the same table, and were served by the same waitress. Hero was a man of routine and discipline and, no matter what else was going on, we never missed a Tuesday meeting. I had begun to rely heavily on these meetings and was grateful that Hero never broke habit.

"What's good, Hero?"

Hero wiped his forehead with the napkin on his lap and smiled slightly. "How's my daughter?"

"As far as I know, she's good. Still working on that business you had her handle."

Hero frowned. "Business? What business?"

"I don't know. She called a couple days ago and told me that she was going out of town on your word to take care of something for you."

Hero fell silent. Now I was wondering what was up. Why did she lie to me? The fuck was she doing out of town if she wasn't doing what she said she was doing?

"Grey, what's going on with store three?" he asked out of the blue.

Damn man! I just knew that nigga Grizzy couldn't keep his mouth closed. I shook my head. "Damn, Grizzy told you about that shit?"

"After some coercion." Hero attempted to laugh but ended up breaking into a coughing fit. I pushed his glass of water towards him.

"Take a sip, man."

Hero took the glass and downed the whole thing. After catching his breath, he continued. "Why did Grizzy have to tell me anyway? Why wouldn't that be something that I would have been made aware of as soon as you found out?"

I sighed. I was getting tired of his bullshit. Hero was the connect, the plug, the resource. He wasn't supposed to be my mothafucking boss! I was my own man! I calmed the rage brewing inside me because I didn't need people to see me lose my cool. "Hero, man. When are you going to let me fly solo? I ain't never seen a connect be so involved with shit," I stated plainly.

"My reputation and freedom is on the line every time a transaction is made. I made a mistake years ago that reminded me that, although I'm am not required to get my hands dirty, sometimes it's very necessary."

"You don't trust me? I can fuck your daughter and walk her down the aisle, but you don't trust me with your business? That's says a lot about where your priorities are."

Hero's normally light-brown colored skin was starting to turn an ashy shade of yellow. I looked on with concern as he wiped his forehead again.

"My daughter is a grown woman. And while I don't like to hear about her getting fucked, that's her business. My money and my product is my business whether it has exchanged hands or not. Thank you for making sure my priorities are straight, though," he smirked.

I chuckled lightly to keep myself from flipping the table over and knocking him in his shit. I flagged over our waitress. She came running quickly, her titties nearly bouncing right out of her shirt. "Aye, we're going to need those drinks sooner rather than later. Oh, and you can bring those crab cakes too."

"No problem, sir."

She smiled before she scurried off, and I smiled to myself. I had been hitting the lil' chick off with a couple racks to poison Hero ever since I found out that he was forcing me to propose to his daughter. It was a slow death, and it was the reason why I had been stalling with Nakami for so long. It was my only option. Hero was always flanked by at least two trained killers at all times, even more when he was at his home or on the road. He had more security than the president.

I had thought about getting some of my foot soldiers to do the work, but they were all loyal to Hero because they had heard or seen what this looney nigga was capable of. Plus, if I wanted to take over his business, I didn't need his niggas knowing that I had their boss slumped. Although this nigga was insane, most of his people were loyal. If they knew that I had killed their leader, nothing would stop them from coming after me. They needed to think that this shit was an accident; his death couldn't be tied to me in any way. Which meant that when the waitress met me tonight to get the last of her money, she was going to be surprised that she received a bullet to the dome instead.

I had tried to hire an outside hit, but as soon as they heard that Hero was the one that I wanted dead, they declined. The nigga was really untouchable. This was the only way for me to get at him. And by the way he looked today, I could tell that it was working. When the waitress came back, thallium would be in his water and inside of his crab cakes. The crab cakes would take a while to digest, so while I was at the crib chilling with my feet up, this nigga would be somewhere taking his last breath. And I couldn't have been happier.

NAKAMI

March 2015

I had been following this bitch for three days, and I was growing hella bored. Today would be the day that I made my presence known. I watched as Blu walked out of the mall with a stupid amount of bags in tow. I had no doubt that she was spending the money that I had so graciously allowed her to make on the baby that was growing inside of her with half of my man's DNA. The thought made me shake with anger, and it took everything in me not to take out the .45 that was in my purse and light the bitch up. But we needed to talk first.

So I hopped into my rental car and followed her. She was staying at the Westin Kierland Spa and Resort, so I had since left my much nicer hotel to lay-up in a chain hotel. Ew. But I needed to have access to the hotel at all times, so I had to bite the bullet. I followed her back to the hotel and watched her take all her things inside. I waited around in the lobby for twenty minutes before I made my way to room 478 to surprise my "best friend."

Butterflies built up in my stomach as I took the elevator up. Despite what I was about to do, I had love for Blu. She was the only other person in my life that had ever meant something to me outside of Grey and my father. Although she had violated me, those feelings of the sisterly bond we used to have still lingered in my heart.

The elevator finally stopped, and I walked off and down the hall to her room. I knocked and then stood to the side of the peephole so that she couldn't see me. A smart person wouldn't have opened the door if they weren't able to determine who was outside. She proved she wasn't that smart when she swung the door wide open.

"Hey boo!" I smiled widely. I didn't wait for her to extend an invitation to come inside; I just pushed right past her.

"Nakami! What...what are you doing here? How did you know I was here?" She closed the door and faced me with a puzzled look on her face.

I hated to admit it, but she looked beautiful. She wasn't showing yet, but her skin was radiant and she looked relaxed and happy. Dressed in a lime green, black, and white Parker dress and black L.A.M.B. wedges, and with her hair in a neat halo braid, she looked almost angelic. *Stupid bitch.*

"Oh, Grey told me that you were coming out here."

"Grey? I didn't tell Grey where I was going."

Damn. I was sure that she had clued her baby daddy in about her whereabouts.

"Fuck this nice shit," I said before I pulled out my .45 with an attached silencer.

"Kami! What the fuck?" She stared at me with wide eyes but didn't move.

"I should be asking you the same thing. When were you going to tell me that you were pregnant?"

"What? He told you?"

"He didn't have to. I walked in on ya'll discussing the bastard baby the other day."

"I...I... I don't understand why you're so upset."

I walked close to Blu and grimaced. This trick had to be kidding me. She was carrying my man's baby, and she didn't know why I was so upset? The thought sent me reeling and, before I knew it, I had slammed the butt of my gun into her head and she dropped.

KIMANI

March 2015

I pounded on Grey's door like I was the fucking police. Someone was going to give me some fucking answers today. I had been to Blu's house every day since Nakami had dropped the bomb on me, and she had been right; Blu had dipped. I called her until my fingers got tired, and I received her voicemail every time. A nigga was beyond frustrated, but I wasn't giving up until I got to the bottom of this.

Shit had gotten too weird since Nakami came over. I woke up the next morning with a slight headache and a sticky dick sitting outside of my pants. That mystery had been solved when I had looked through my phone and found the video of Nakami and me fucking. Or should I say of Nakami fucking me. I was out cold. Bitch must have slipped something in my drink. I guess that was her get back for Grey knocking up her bestie, but shit, I didn't want any part of that. Grey was still my brother regardless of what he did, and I just wasn't cut like that.

I banged on the door again and waited a few more seconds before my phone rang. It was Grey.

"Fuck you at?" I barked.

"On my way home. Why?" he answered.

"I'm at your crib."

"Oh, ok. I'll be there in five."

I hung up without saying another word because I had another call coming it. It was blocked, and I was hoping that it was Blu.

"Yo."

"Damn still the same, huh?"

Fuck. "What do you want, Vicious?"

"A chance to make it up to you. I'm sorry, I swear I am," she whined. I was losing my patience with everything and everyone, including her.

"What part of 'I don't fuck with you' don't you get? You're messy, bro. And I'm good."

"So you really want to be with that stripper bitch?" she asked, sucking her teeth.

"How you know?"

"Baby, please. You don't make a move that I don't know about. I can't believe that you would rather lay-up with that used pussy hoe instead of me. She's just a trick bitch looking for a come up."

I had heard enough. I disconnected the call and turned my phone on vibrate. I wasn't in the mood for shit unless it involved the answers to my questions. I paced the winding driveway for a few minutes before Grey's Audi R8 came speeding in. He parked and hopped out, walking towards me with a smile on his face. "What's up, bro?"

"You tell me."

He unlocked the front door and walked inside. I followed him.

"What's that supposed to mean?" he asked.

"You just out here getting bitches pregnant?"

Grey stopped walking and turned around to face me. He looked shook. Guess keeping a secret that big will do that to you. "Nakami is pregnant? How do you know?"

I laughed at this nigga's attempt to deflect. "Naw, nigga. Blu is, though."

His expression changed from worried to confused. "Yeah, I know that. But what does that have to do with me?"

"How would you even know she was pregnant unless you was the one that knocked her up?!" I screamed. His nonchalance was pissing me off.

"The fuck I look like?" He looked at me like I was crazy. "Why would I be fucking Blu?" I asked.

"The same reason you would have been fucking Ginae," I spat.

That shut him up. He didn't think I knew about him lowkey sexing my old chick, but I did. I didn't want to believe that he had went there again with Blu, but apparently I shouldn't put anything past him.

"Look man, that was on some drunk shit. She came on to me, and I tried to get her to stop but she-"

"That shit is old, bruh. But you know how I feel about Blu. Why would you even…" I couldn't even talk anymore. I could feel myself getting choked up and angry, and I didn't even want to go there.

"I didn't! Where are you getting this from?"

"Nakami. She heard ya'll talking the other day at the club. And she came and told me."

"She…what?! Oh, fuck. Man, no." He walked into his office and I followed him. "Blu came to tell me about the pregnancy, but that's your kid."

"Look, I know about it now. You ain't gotta lie. Just tell me why, bro."

"I'm not lying. Look." Grey pulled up his laptop and hit a few buttons. He spun the computer around and it displayed a video from his club. He hit the space bar and the video started to play. I watched as he and Blu walked out to the patio and listened as Blu spilled her feelings to him about the baby and me. I couldn't help the tears that escaped when I realized that I actually had a kid on the way by the woman I loved. I couldn't believe this shit.

The video came to an end, and I looked up at Grey. "Man, I'm…"

"Aye, I'm sorry bro. About Ginae and never telling you about that shit. That was wrong. And I shouldn't have hid this stuff about Blu from you either."

"You good. But why would Nakami think that the kid was yours?"

"Who knows? You know the broad ain't right upstairs."

Suddenly I thought about the video and the text that she sent me. I felt horrible. I know that she had drugged me, but I had still stuck my dick in her and that shit shouldn't have went down.

"Aye, I gotta show you something," I sighed. I took my phone out and showed the text and video to Grey. "I'm sorry, bruh. That bitch drugged me though!"

"You having sex with her isn't a big deal. You know that she on her way outta there anyway, but what is this shit she's talking in the text message? 'I knew you wouldn't get the revenge we deserved, so I did it for you. People don't cross me and get away scott free.' Fuck is that about?"

"I don't even know, man. And to be honest, I don't care. I just want to find Blu and make this right."

Grey paced the floor. "I don't know where she is. She told me she was out, but never said where she was going."

"Damn."

We sat in silence for a moment. Suddenly, Grey stopped in his tracks. He then turned around to me. "You know what's crazy? Nakami called a few days ago and told me that she had to go out of town to do something for her father. But when I talked to him today, he had no clue what I was talking about. You don't think she would try to hurt Blu, do you?"

"If anybody would have known where Blu ran off to, it would have been Nakami. Maybe she went to talk to her? She seemed pretty upset when I talked to her the other day."

"I don't know, man. If she thinks that Blu is carrying my seed, there is no telling what she might do."

"Fuck!" I grabbed my head and started pacing in a circle. "What are we going to do? I can't let anything happen to her, man!"

"Hey, calm down. We'll figure this out."

"Grey, my nigga, Nakami and Blu have been gone for three days already. There is no telling what already has gone down, and we don't even know where she's at!" I started to get frantic. I was useless if I couldn't protect the people I loved.

"Well, if Nakami really did go to find Blu, I know how we can find them."

"You ain't said nothing but a word, nigga. How?"

BLU

March 2015

My eyes fluttered open and I try to adjust my eyes to see in the dark. It was dark, with only a dim flicker from the broken ceiling light and from the crack in the boarded up window, providing a hazy view of my surroundings. I could tell it was dark outside. I began to move but realized that my legs and feet were tied to something and I couldn't get free. The taut tape that covered my mouth prevented me from screaming, but it didn't prevent me from freaking out. I rattled and shook until the chair that I was tied to fell over. A muffled scream escaped from my lips when I realized that I had landed next to a dead body. The man's eyes were wide open and held the same terror I was feeling. There was a bullet hole in the middle of his forehead the size of a dime. I didn't know where I was at and how I got there, but I had to get out.

But before I could make another move, I heard a door open and shut. I held my breath as I waited for my abductor to come into view. The lights flickered on, and I almost peed myself when I saw who I had come face to face with. Looking like she had walked straight off the runway, Nakami sashayed into the house with a bright smile on her face. She was dressed like she was going on a date, but she had a paper grocery bag in her hand that she sat on the table and a jug of what looked like gasoline in her other hand. She smiled at the fear that was evident in my eyes and walked over to turn my chair right side up.

"Sorry about the mess. I'm just a terrible housekeeper. But you knew that," she laughed.

I looked around and counted two more dead bodies scattered around the room. I had the urge to throw up but held it in for fear of choking on my own vomit.

"You know everything about me. You know that I would never be caught dead in last season's clothes, that I used to fuck women for sport, that I despise liars, and that I honor loyalty. You are, after all, my best friend. You know me like the back of your hand," she smirked. "So why…why oh why…would you fuck my fiancé?" she asked.

I started trying to talk but remembered the tape was on my mouth. She had really lost her mind. What was she talking about?

"Oh, I want to hear what you have to say. So I'm going to take the tape off, but I will not hesitate to put a bullet in you if you scream." She pulled the gun from the back of her black Hudson jeans and let it rest at her side. "Nod if you understand."

I nodded slowly. She approached me and ripped the tape off my mouth like she would win an award for speed. I flinched, but I'd be damned if I'd give this crazy hoe the satisfaction of knowing that she hurt me.

"So tell me why."

"I didn't."

Nakami shook her head. "So you're really going to lie to my face right now? While I have a gun?"

"I'm not lying, you crazy bitch! I never slept with Grey! I love his brother!" I screamed.

Before I knew what happened, a loud pop filled the air and a sharp pain shot through my arm. I screamed from the pain, and Nakami quickly put another piece of tape over my mouth.

"Keep calling me crazy, and we're going to play this game I like to play called how many bullets. The object is to see how many bullet wounds you can sustain before you bleed out."

What the fuck?! I knew that my homegirl had a few screws loose, but the person standing in front of me was sadistic. Gone was the sister who had come to my rescue and befriended me when no one else would. She had been replaced by a monster. The crazy thing was I didn't know why she thought I slept with Grey. I would never do something like that to her.

"I had a sneaking suspicion that you were jealous of me, but I never thought you would take it this far." She laughed as she unscrewed the cap to the gasoline bucket. "I thought that, as friends, I did everything I could to make sure that you had what I had, or something close to it. But I guess you wanted the real thing."

She started to pour gasoline on the body of the dead man in front of me. I screamed against the tape because I could see what was going to happen. I didn't want to die, especially over a misunderstanding. In that moment I knew that I wanted to live. That I wanted the life that was growing inside of me. I wanted Kimani. I was so sure of everything that I wanted. Why couldn't I have been this sure a few days ago and told Kimani instead of Grey?

Nakami noticed that I was struggling to speak, so she walked over and pulled the tape off again. "What bitch?"

"Why? Why would I be jealous of you? You're my friend. My only friend. Why would I fuck that up over a guy?"

"People have crossed their mother for less, so how would I know?" she growled.

"I don't want Grey. I want Kimani. This is his baby. Please, don't do this," I pleaded.

"You think those crocodile tears are going to move me? I've seen better acting on a telenovela. "

My worry and angst began to turn into anger as I thought about her crazy and illogical thinking. I don't know if it was the pain from the bullet in my arm or the pain from the thought of losing my life over some bullshit, but I lashed out. If I was going to die, she need to hurry up and kill me. Fuck this burning in a house fire bullshit.

"You're really a crazy bitch. I thought you were a few letters short of the alphabet, but damn! You're really going to kill me over a nigga? And a nigga who don't even want your ass no more."

"Shut up! Shut up, bitch! You don't know what you're talking about!"

"Everyone knows that Grey is over your dramatic ass. Kimani told me that your father made him propose to you to keep his business going. Tell me that ain't pathetic. You 'bout to kill your best friend over a nigga who was forced to fuck with you," I laughed wildly. I was starting to feel a little lightheaded and woozy, but I kept laughing until I felt it. My eyes shot open in shock as I realized I had been shot again. I looked down and saw the blood pouring out of my stomach, and I wanted to cry. I didn't have the time. I felt my head rolling around, and I swore I saw Kimani and Grey before I felt my soul leave my body and everything turn dark.

GREY

March 2015

"Noooooooooooo!" Hearing the scream coming from my brother's mouth tore at my heart. I watched as he rushed over to Blu's limp body and held her. I wanted to be there for my brother, but I needed to get at Nakami first. She aimed her gun at me with wide eyes and shaky hands as I trained my gun at her head.

"Grey, what are you doing?" she asked with fear and confusion illuminating her eyes.

"What does it look like I'm doing, bitch? I'm about to take care of a problem I should have taken care of a long time ago."

We had used Nakami's phone to track her down in Phoenix. We hopped the jet and made it to Arizona in time to catch Nakami running errands. I had Kimani follow her while I hit up a few of our workers to see if we could find Blu. We used every resource we had. The trail stopped at the Westin hotel, where she had purchased a room for two weeks. I linked back up with Kimani around 3 pm and had been trailing Nakami ever since.

We followed her around from the mall, to the grocery store, and to the hardware store, waiting for her to lead us to Blu. Imagine my surprise when I found out she was holed up in one of my trap houses. When she went in, we surveyed the house and were surprised to see that the bitch had taken out the whole trap. After we made sure she didn't have any help, we moved in.

"She meant that much to you? That baby and that bitch meant that much that you're going to kill your fiancé over it? Fuck her!"

She waved the gun wildly and my brother hopped up with the quickness, firing two shots; one landed in her leg and the other landed in her arm. The bullet to her leg sent her crashing to the ground. She landed on the floor, dropping the gun to grab at her wounds. She let out a gut-wrenching scream. Carefully, I stepped closer to Kimani and where the gun had slid.

"No, fuck you, you lunatic ass bitch! Do you know what you just did? Huh?" I could see my brother unraveling, and it hurt me to my core.

"Aye, Mani. Get Blu and take her to the hospital. Let me handle this. Please." I put one hand on top of his and pushed the gun down out of Nakami's face, while I still had my piece aimed at her. Tears continued to fall from his eyes, as he nodded slowly and walked over to Blu. I continued to aim and stare at Nakami, who was also crying, until Kimani walked pasted me carrying Blue and I heard Kimani close the door. Quickly, I picked up the gun she had dropped and shoved it in the back of my jeans.

"Grey, please," Nakami begged.

"Fuck all that. You really killed your best friend over me? You are a dumb bitch. And to think that I felt a little bad about having to kill you."

"Wha...what?" She shook like a leaf.

"See, the thing is...you're fucking crazy. And I've put up with your bullshit for way too long. All the drama. The damaged cars, the torn and bleached clothes, the broken electronics. All that shit done based off of some imaginary shit you've concocted in that tiny ass brain of yours." I tapped the gun against her forehead and she flinched.

Carefully, I walked over towards where the gasoline can had fallen and picked it up. I started to douse Nakami in what was left. She screamed bloody murder.

"You just killed your best friend, and your niece or nephew. Fucking killed them! I never had sex with Blu. Not a day in my life and never would have. But you just had to jump the gun before you got facts. Like always."

"So you're going to kill me, Grey? My father will fucking-"

I cut her off. "Oh, yeah I forgot to tell you. Your father died a few hours ago. I was tired of him too. The apple doesn't fall far from the tree. I would have hated to know ya moms."

Nakami tried to lunge for me, but I stuck the gun out even further to make sure she knew I wasn't playing. She couldn't get far on that leg Kimani had shot her in anyway.

"Sit that ass back down, girl. You ain't going nowhere. You made your bed, and now you're going to lie in it." I took her arm and dragged her to the back of the room to make sure she couldn't get out. I pulled out my lighter and flicked it open. A flame ignited, and I started to feel euphoric. I was about to be free of this miserable bitch, and knowing it felt damn good. It was too bad that I had to lose a niece or nephew and my brother had to lose another girlfriend.

"Grey…stop! I love you! Please!" Nakami begged for her life, but her pleas fell on deaf ears. I was sick of her ruining my life and destroying everything around me. It was the final thing I had to do to start my life again. So I took a piece of the mail that was on the counter and lit it.

"Grey…nooooooooooooo!"

I dropped the paper on the floor and watched for a moment as the whole wall went up in flames. Nakami tried to scoot out the way; she even tried to stand. But it was useless. Her leg was too fucked up, and she couldn't pull strength from the arm she had gotten shot in. I smirked as I watched her struggle. No longer entertained, I turned around and walked away. Nakami's bloodcurdling screams filled the air as I walked out the door and shut it closed. You may think I'm a monster, but I don't give a fuck. Nakami had crossed the line, and she got what she deserved. Now I was free to live life in peace with her burning in hell.

NAKAMI

June 2015

My eyes shot open, and I could feel my heart beating out of my chest. Anxiety blanketed me as I realized I was familiar with my surroundings. Where the fuck was I? I tried to move, but pain engulfed my entire body when I attempted to make the smallest move. There were bandages everywhere and tubes and wires attached to my body with the opposite sides attached to a bunch of beeping machines. The room was large and bright with two bay windows on either side. The room was decorated to a tee by someone with very expensive taste. There were two arm chairs on the other side of the room that were well over a rack a piece and the wallpaper on the wall was at least three-hundred and fifty dollars a yard. There were two doors on the left side; one open and one closed. The open door gave way to what looked like a well decorated bedroom.

What the entire fuck?

The closed door opened and a short, dark skinned woman dressed in lime green scrubs walked into the room. She was wheeling a metal cart with a bunch of things on them. When she noticed I was awake, she smiled.

"Good morning, Miss. Glad to see you're finally awake."

"Where the hell am I?" I croaked. My throat burned like acid had been poured down it.

"You're in Atlanta, ma'am."

"I mean…where? How did I get here? What happened?"

The nurse walked around my bed and pressed some buttons on one of the beeping machines. A long receipt printed out before she answered. "Don't worry, you're safe. And you're getting treatment for your injuries."

I looked at her skeptically. None of this made sense.

"I'm Nadine, and my boss saved you from a house fire that you were in. You were barely alive when he pulled you out, and you slipped into a coma from all of the trauma to your body. You were out for about two and a half months, girl. On top of that, you sustained multiple gunshots and third degree burns from your face to your feet."

Tears pooled as I listened to her continue to ramble. Everything came flooding back to me. Me killing my best friend, Grey and Kimani coming to her rescue, Kimani shooting me, and Grey lighting the house on fire. It all came rushing back. Before I could stop myself, I lifted my upper body from the throng of pillows behind me.

The nurse noticed and quickly came to my aid. "Whoa, there! You can't…"

I ignored her as I continued to get up from the bed. The pain was damn near unbearable, but the thought of all that had transpired hurt even worse. I ripped the cords and tubes from my body, and Nadine ran over to the machines and struggled to keep them from falling to the floor. I noticed the mirror on the far side of the room, and I slowly walked towards it. When I finally approached the mirror, I was mortified at what I saw. Most of my head was wrapped in bandages but, from what I saw, I wanted to throw up. My face was completely unrecognizable and covered in horrifying burns. I had no eyebrows and, from what I could tell, no hair either. I began to shake with anger as I gripped the buffet table in front of me for support. Infuriated, I picked up the vase full of flowers in front of me.

I watched as the glass vase I had been holding in my hand soared through the air, crashed landed against the white croc skin wallpaper, and burst into a million pieces. Tears rained down my disfigured face, burning my open wounds as I tried to come to grips with what had just happened.

"Ma'am …you're not in any condition to be moving around," the nurse timidly stated. I whipped around so forcefully that my neck made a popping noise.

"Bitch, if you don't get the fuck out my business, you're going to be the next thing that goes flying across this fucking room. Now piss off!" I roared. Without another word, she ran her ass up out the room, heeding my warning.

"How could this have happened? Why would he do this?" I dropped to my knees and landed right on a pile of broken glass. The glass cut into my flesh, immediately causing blood to leak all over the mahogany wood floors. The pain of the open wounds felt like the cusp of an orgasm in comparison to the unbearable pain I felt in my heart.

Rage wasn't a strong enough word to describe the feeling coursing through my body. It was something worse than that. Deadlier than that. The feeling was consuming me, eating me alive from the inside out. It was awakening a dark side of me that no one, including me, had ever borne witness to.

Stumbling, I rose from the broken glass and limped to my room. During the short trip from the mirror to my bed, I thought about the possible ways I could make him suffer twelve times over. Letting gunshots ring off and hit his body like Fourth of July fireworks wouldn't be satisfying enough. Drawing blood by stabbing him directly in the heart as he had stabbed me—metaphorically speaking, of course—would be too swift. No, he needed to be dealt with in a specific manner. He needed to have everything in his life stripped from him and be forced to live with the daily reminder that he was the one that brought this on himself. The gauntlet had been thrown, and I wasn't going to stop until the nigga that I'd given my heart to had his ripped out and hung on a wall like a trophy of vengeance won.

to be continued...

To receive a text when part 2 of this book is released, text the keyword "Jessica" to 25827.

About the author:

Originally born in Detroit, MI, Bri moved to Ann Arbor, MI with her family when she was 11. In high school she was introduced to the world of urban fiction when she read "The Coldest Winter Ever" and was hooked! She started writing her own short stories and novels soon after.

After she graduated Huron High School in 05, she attended Central State University and from there went on to graduate with an Associate's Degree from Washtenaw Community College. After leaving WCC, she attended Eastern Michigan University where she majored in Theatre Arts.

After taking a screenwriting class and falling in love with a new form or writing, she moved to Los Angeles to pursue a career in screenwriting. Being and a new city with a refreshed state of mind, sparked a few ideas that led to a full-fledged novel. After reading a novel by Jessica Watkins called Secrets of a Side Bitch, she was inspired to submit what she was working on and the rest is history! *Long As You Know Who You Belong To* is her first published novel. :)

Follow her on:

Instagram: bri_noreen
Facebook: facebook.com/brinoreen
Website: authorbrinorren.wix.com/brinoreen

Made in the USA
Charleston, SC
16 September 2016